The Rabbit Saga Colle...

#vampire #serialkiller #thriller

MALCONTENT

emil jersey

Malcontent
By Emil Jersey
First Edition, ©2020 by Emil Jersey

ISBN-13: 9781734047448
Also available in eBook

Run Rabbit Books
Imprint of Little Roni Publishers, LLC
www.littleronipublishers.com/run-rabbit-books.php
v.07052021

Send inquiries regarding this novel to the editor,
submissionslrp@gmail.com

www.EmilJersey.com

PUBLISHED IN THE UNITED STATES OF AMERICA

Run Rabbit Books
New Adult General Adult Imprint of Little Roni Publishers, LLC

From the Author:

Your author used to be a Rakum (you would call us "vampires"), but our world changed forever when we woke up one night transformed into mortals.

This book is a fictionalized account of real events that happened to my brothers in 2019.

I read a thread in our chatroom entitled, "Pitch and the Psychotherapist," and followed it for laughs. When my beloved Darcy's name began to be tossed around, I took interest. When he began to play a role in the resolution of the problems that arose, I decided to write this novel.

That said, some of this is true and some of it is bullshit. All of it is magnificent fun, so enjoy.

~ Jersey

Emil Jersey, Athens, GA 2019

TABLE OF CONTENTS

The Therapist

I can't call him Pitch. I hate that name—sounds like the devil. Tonight, I asked if I could call him Rich or Richard. He said why don't I call him "Jackass Loser Shit-head" instead, because it would have the same meaning to his people.

His people.

I've been aware of the Rakum for eleven years. That means I knew about them before they were mortal, and that means I used to be a Cow.[1] Anyone aware of the Rakum can appreciate why I'm mortified to write those words.

Doctor Ruth Laura Angleton used to be a Cow.

What certified and licensed psychotherapist would voluntarily give her body and blood to any Rakum that crossed her path? No sane person would melt at the sight of her master, lift both wrists and bear her breasts in the hopes he might take her blood and her sex altogether.

I raise my hand. I was that woman. There is no rational explanation.

Wait.

---

[1] "Rakum Cow": Before the Rakum lost their birthright, a Cow was a mortal viscerally drawn to the Rakum to serve in whatever way he desired.

Keifer gave me an explanation a few months into our relationship.

Keifer—*Kfir* is what his people call him—is a Rakum I met a year ago, which means *after* they went human. He explained that since the beginning of time, there had been a Rakum spirit inside all his people, and because of a gigantic "work of God," that spirit was exorcised, sent away forever. When that happened, he and his brethren turned human. They call this event (ominously, I might add), "11/13," since this spiritual battle took place on November 13, 2018. I had lost my "Cow-ness" after an earlier Rakum battle with the spirit world, so when Keifer and I met, I was drawn to him *as a man,* an extremely sexy man, but it was natural, not supernatural.

On with journaling tonight's session with Pitch.

Pitch, Session 2, 7pm, Friday

True-Client Software™ **bolds Client's spoken word**
MedVR™ transcripts used to populate dialog and build this entry
Loc: My office on 27th Ave

Pre-Notes: Recall, he selected the hard-backed wooden chair last session.

"Don't wear that shit perfume when I visit, eh?"

Pitch's greeting didn't surprise me, and I waited for him to sit. Tonight, he chose to pace a circuit before my desk. I chose this furniture with his type in mind—the type that moves constantly. The desk butted against the wall provides five feet of solid wood between me and the client, with a credenza on my right preventing any incoming traffic. My exit strategy is a straight line to the office door, so if he were to block it; heck, I don't know.

"Tell me how it went last night," I asked. He had scheduled a job interview with a security company. He glared and shook his head as if I was the biggest idiot he'd ever seen.

"Why the fuck do I need a job? I could buy that company seventy-times over."

I guess he didn't get it or didn't go. He was right about the money; the Rakum that survived 11/13 each inherited twenty million dollars from their dead leaders' coffers. Pitch rented a luxury condo in town, but Keifer said his main residence was on a vast tract of farmland in Columbus, Mississippi, in a fully-restored, white-columned plantation house. He moved here to keep tabs on Keifer who had been his roommate before we met. In fact, Pitch came to me on advice from Keifer. They came from the same pack[2] and had been compatible. But more on that later. Considering the Rakum's scowl, I wondered which question to ask next. Which provocation was most likely to deliver the outcome I sought?

"Tell me what happened," I said watching him pace the room. He knew I found him attractive, and not because I used to be a Cow. He read my countenance and maybe my body language. Since he is two-hundred and nineteen years old, it's safe to assume he knows what I'm thinking most of the time. Keifer said they studied mortals like I might study a favorite hobby.

I waited for him to answer and let my eyes do their

---

[2] Rakum are grouped in "packs" led by one of the 100 Elders. This becomes a lifelong identifier. Pitch and Kfir both came from Elder Bel's pack.

3

thing. I'd never ogle a normal patient, but my Rakum clients expect me to be straightforward. Part of that is not hiding my thoughts. Thus, I bare it all. They have no embarrassment, no modesty, no shyness, and they prefer I play that role, too, as best as I can.

"If you let your hair down, you wouldn't look like such a frigid bitch," he said then and stopped moving to lean both palms on the desk facing me. **"How long is it? Show me."**

I held his eye evenly and I reached behind my head to squeeze open the jaws of my jumbo alligator clip. My hair is powerful—thick, long, brown with golden highlights expertly added by my stylist. Keifer calls it my mane, so I unfurled it with style and flipped it loose, using my hands to arrange the thick halves over each shoulder. I know from studying it in the mirror that it has the most power this way. I licked my lips and gave Pitch a languid eye. The corner of his mouth turned up the tiniest bit and his deep hazel eyes grew darker.

"Fuck, yeah," he said in a near whisper and stood off the desk to step to my only exit.

He stopped in place making it obvious he wanted me to step closer. He wanted to touch my hair. Keifer told me Pitch wouldn't hurt me—not even a little—that they had a pact between brothers, so if I trusted Kiefer, I could trust Pitch. Because of this, I stepped from behind the desk.

"You and Keifer tight?" he asked, and his right hand lifted to touch the surface, stroking as if it were a kitten. Then his left hand lifted, and he used his fingers to run the length of it, from my ears to the ends. When he ran out of hair, he dove back in, the odd smile growing, and he pushed the whole of it behind my shoulders. He smelled good, aftershave and an Irish-Spring-type bar soap, both I

4

find pleasing.

"Does he fuck you with his eyes closed?"

I was not provoked. There are therapy models for humans and an entirely different set for Rakum. I developed their model over the past two years, using personality types of my extreme cases and a few official law enforcement, FBI, and AMA public-education databases. Another therapist (Heather, from the transcript) feeds the spreadsheet when she has a Rakum client. We came up with a fine program for these guys, and trust me, with Rakum, expect them to say anything. The trick is to remember it is meaningless.

"Do you want to talk about my sex life or your experience yesterday?"

Pitch sucked his teeth in a slow manner, his eyes on my hair and his hands now petting it as one might a magnificent stallion, with reverence and awe. I studied the curve of his throat beneath his trimmed beard. He groomed with great care and I did not hide my scrutiny.

"Let's do both. You answer whatever I ask and I'll do the same."

"Fine," I replied and waited for him to go first. In our previous (and introductory) session, he hadn't answered any questions. I spent the hour talking and he wouldn't look at me. I was surprised he came back, but Keifer said he would (it's good to have an inside man).

"Does Keifer fuck you in the ass?" Pitch asked, and I could see he thought he had me with that one. But he didn't. Before I began my reply, he added, **"Because you know he prefers his brothers."**

I smiled at that, which I guess he didn't expect. What he didn't know is that Keifer quizzed me on these sorts of questions. Keifer's been in some very dark places, mentally and corporeally, so much of what he prepared me for if I was going to work with the Rakum was difficult to imagine. Same-sex relations was easy.

"No, we do not engage in anal sex," I answered in a forensic manner. I hoped it would encourage him to also be more scientific, but...

"Let me check that box for you, Doc. I promise to take it easy. I make my own lube and I'll go slow."

"Tell me what happened yesterday regarding the job interview."

Tit for tat. I was still standing in front of him and he dropped contact with my hair. He looked left, swiveled away, and paced to the soft cushioned chair on the near wall. He dropped into it with a noisy exhale and regarded me. Now he was too far away for my feminine-therapist wiles to be effective, so I went to sit catty-corner on a similar chair five feet away.

"Okay, Doc, but you've heard my next question; be thinking of a good answer."

He shoved himself several inches into the cushion which caused his knees to hang open before him on the thick carpet. He's taller than Keifer, maybe 6'3", and built very much the same, muscular, athletic, like a baseball player in the prime of his career. Even in his indigo-blue jeans, I noted thighs that pressed the fabric, begging to be less encumbered.

My eyes were too low and Pitch snapped his fingers at chest level. I pretended it was no big deal and he started his reply.

"I arrived on time and the supervisor wasn't in. They asked me to wait in reception and a tiny blonde female sat there waiting. She was half your age, half your size, a million times prettier, and I talked her into

sneaking into the executive lounge where I bent her over the sink and introduced her to my people."

"You had sex?" I asked him and he smiled, this time using the grin mortals hate—the one that says, *when you least expect it, I'll bite your nose off.*

"Now you want to talk about my sex life? Excellent."

"My question is still in play. You're telling me what happened at the interview."

"That was it. I fucked her in the boss's loo. He came in, his timing perfect. My last two or three thrusts, he stepped in and focused his eyes. I didn't pull out. I held Miss Tiny real tight. The boss shouted for security. I came and I fastened my pants. Security escorted me to the front door. The end."

I held Pitch's gaze a few long seconds and he held his face static. He wanted me to have a natural female reaction, but as I stated before, Keifer's preparations were very thorough.

"The young woman vouched for you and no police were involved. Plus, the interview never happened. Got it."

He smiled and looked as if I surprised him. I made a note on my pad and he asked me what I wrote. I said, is that your next question, and he shook his head.

"I don't give a shit; write whatever you want. My question is, if Keifer told you to do it, would you have sex with me?"

Dammit, he surprised me. I was unable to hide my widened eyes, giving him a victory. My brain sought a pithy and meaningless answer, but the only replies that came to mind took him seriously. Was he going to ask Keifer such a ridiculous thing? And what would my beloved answer? He'd never agree, right?

Pitch looked at his phone and stood. I got up, too. He still had fifteen minutes on the clock.

"See you Wednesday, Doc," he said and shot me a new look, one with the sultry bedroom eyes all his brethren possess. **"I got plans."**

I countered and followed him out, but nothing I said kept him in the building. At my office elevator, he stepped in backwards, waving his fingers. As the door began its closing, he held up his hands, poking one finger into a hole made by those on his other hand.

"OUCH! Shit, Pitch! Not there! FUCK!" he said in a high voice and the door thunked shut.

End Session Notes

The Transcript

Private Chat / BessemerMentalHealth.org (BMH)
Topic: **RKM SERIAL KILLER**
Thread title: **Patient07 Rape/Torture/Souvenir** (tongue)
Thread Owner: Ruth Angleton, PhD
Participants (in italics): Heather Flank, PhD

: You saw the paper last night? The trans woman in Jemison?

: uh oh

: He's claiming it. Get this. He jerked off while he was telling me.

: No way. Wait—I believe it. My guy would jerk off in my office if I let my guard down.

: It was horrible. It'd give you nightmares. I want to tell the police or someone...

: You know you can't and don't worry—they'll find her. Did he say he left her like the others?

: ...

: Was she raped in post-mortem stab wounds?

: *He didn't mention that precisely, but he described raping her in a field in, quote, all orifices. It's gotta be him, right? I need to tell—*

: No! Just keep listening. Make notes for our project. Do not tell ANYONE. You know better. STOP THINKING ABOUT TELLING THE POLICE! You can't break confidentiality with RKM. You knew that going in. If you do, expect to orphan your daughter. I'm sorry, but it's true.

: ...

: Are you crying?

: *Jesus, Ruth. I won't say anything, shit. But you didn't hear him. He loves killing so much! He spoke of it like you might speak of Keifer or how I might speak of my daughter. He loves torturing these women so very much!*

: You're doing a great job. Hang in there, okay?

: ...

: Heather? Is he being truthful or is he manipulating you?

: *I'm not sure. He's still calling-in his sessions. I can't watch his body language or read his countenance.*

: That's probably why he won't come in person.

: *I thought of that, but what can I do? I want to help him figure this out. And the data I'm getting off his case—it's really piling up.*

10

malcontent

: You're uploading it to our spreadsheet, right?

: *Every session. Tell me what you think of this—the papers said the killer is taking tongues. Did you see that?*

: The tip of the tongue is severed and not at the crime scene.

: *Yeah. Pt07 didn't mention tongues for three weeks. Brags about each rape in detail, but nothing about tongues. This week, he said he snips off the tip of the tongue with a cigar trimmer. He told me the brand and everything. Did he make that up? See it in the paper and claim it because I'm such a good listener?*

: Huh, it is important for them to feel superior. But consider the model; they don't lie about sex or violence.

: *I know. I know. Another thing. He has never mentioned post-mortem penetration.*

: Why would he hold that back? Rhetorical question. I know. Tell me; is it time for a provocation?

: …

: We have a model.

: …

: Heather?

: *I'm dreading it, but, yes, I have it in my notes to provoke him next session. He might stop calling-in, but*

: Then that's on him.

: I guess. Okay, I'm logging off. TTYL

END

... *"There's my little sugar cookie," Daddy said and none of his words had edges. He was drunk. My forehead prickled with nervousness. I couldn't get past him, he took up the entire doorway. He was reaching for me, telling me how sweet I smelled. "Daddy's good little cookie," he said in my ear and picked me up to take me to his room where he would set up his video camera...*

The Ballet

as it the latest Rakum transcript that gave me that nightmare? God, who knows. Nonetheless, I no longer journal bad dreams. When I was in therapy, I kept track of all of them. Now if an old memory worked itself into a dream, I had methods of repressing it before I put my feet to the floor. This morning, it was tucked back into its locked-down file folder and I concentrated on the sculpted tattooed arms around my middle.

Keifer said his name means "lion" and it suits him. He's regal, strong, kind, and beautiful. I'm aware one of those is not a Rakum attribute, but he saw a therapist before we met and found balance.

This morning he awoke before I did and snuggled into my body from behind, his thick arms encircling my ribcage. I sleep in panties and a tank top so I can truly enjoy the sensation of him tucking his forearms beneath my breasts and pulling our bodies together all the way down. I responded by turning my head for a kiss. He's not offended by odors, so he never cares if I have brushed my teeth or showered. (For the record, I shower daily, *ahem.*)

Tucked between my cheeks, his good morning is growing, pressing for attention, and there is nothing more I want in the world right then than for him to come all the way in. And he did—the way I'm accustomed, not Pitch's way—and I was sorry the creep came to mind when his total opposite lovingly touched me in all the ways I desired. When we had both reached a very happy end, he lay on his back, grinning, sweating, and now and then, saying, "Oh-boy," like a high school nerd. I folded into him and he held me with one arm, my cheek to his chest.

"Pitch told me about your session," Keifer said after a quiet moment, his voice neutral. "Do you want to have sex with him?"

He didn't look at my face when he asked his preposterous question as a mortal man would have. Nothing Keifer did was normal and I had grown accustomed to it.

"No, I don't want him to touch me," I replied, choosing my words because Keifer takes everything literally. "I expect he'll always try to provoke me with sexual innuendo, but no, *never* do I want to touch him or have him touch me. Can you make that clear to him?" I propped up to read Keifer's eyes and only then did he turn his face to mine.

"He will not touch you unless you consent." Keifer's expression showed nothing. He had stated a fact. There was nothing else to say or do.

"Good," I said finally and relaxed against him. "What did he tell you about me?"

Keifer is never embarrassed and will answer anything, so I knew to only ask what I could handle to hear.

"He loves looking at your hair. He doesn't like the wrinkles on either side of your mouth. He spends a lot of time fantasizing what you look like nude, especially from behind."

He tilted his chin so I peeked upward. He was grinning

and he squeezed me once. "He said you wore really tight slacks last night and your Pilates is working."

I felt my cheeks flush, mostly because Keifer's expression said he agreed on the last point. I wasn't petite and had always been most comfortable in a 10 or 12, but the Rakum like a woman with a little meat. As for smile wrinkles? Thank goodness I have them. Life is tough and I never had it easy. Plus, Keifer and Pitch have a supernatural reason to look barely thirty. I fought and struggled my way through thirty years of *real life*. I earned more than a few lines on my face.

We didn't say more about it. Over the past two years, I've helped five Rakum deal with their anger at becoming mortal against their will. Pitch is the only one so far that has been vile—the others were sad and tragic, but they grasped within a week the ideas I put forward to help them move to the next level. Pitch was going to take longer. I hope I can hang in there. Yes. I will hang in there.

"Have you ever seen a cotton boll?" Kiefer asked a few moments later. My brain was fuzzy and I figured I misheard.

"Like for removing makeup?"

"No, a *boll*. A crusty ball at the end of the cotton stalk. Inside is *cotton.*"

He sounded amazed and I hadn't given cotton plants much thought. It was pretty incredible; I mean, a plant that makes clothing?

"I don't think I've ever held one. You saw some on your drive?"

"In a field on highway 31."

Ah. 31 runs parallel to I-65, and every Southern traveler knows it to be a beautiful countryside route of farms and small towns.

15

"Let's see," I replied, the map in my head running down the roads. "Prattville, Clanton, Jemison… Did you go north or south?"

I listened for his reply, but he fell still. He doesn't work and spends his free time visiting his brothers. Sometimes he takes long drives that last an entire day. We always wake up in the same bed, but if he drives far enough out, he'll tip-toe into bed before dawn. The Rakum have very active minds so I encourage whatever he can do to keep it pumping. When they get bored, they get into trouble, which was another reason I decided to focus my practice on their brethren. Anger isn't their only issue.

I rolled onto my side and my lover completed the spoon. I nearly dozed off, Keifer's body heat providing the most delicious cocoon a woman could ask for. Before I was full asleep, he asked about Heather.

"Has she said anything else about Patient 7?" he asked further molding his front to my back.

He worried for his brother—before they lost their Rakum-ness, they had all been attached by a mystical tether. This made them *brethren* in a much larger way than we can understand. They didn't share blood across their race—there had been ten main leaders that contributed sperm to create their people—but they shared the Rakum spirit I mentioned before. This spirit is what made them supernatural. It's cool stuff to talk about now, but when they were living it, they had no idea whence their power came.

But I digress trying to explain why Keifer worried so much about a patient he didn't know. Then again, he *might* know him. There had been 100,000 Rakum before things went south. To answer, I rolled onto my back to see his face and shared everything she said in Tuesday's BMH

16

chat. I ended with, "He didn't say anything about the tongues until this week."

"Tongues?" he said in a soft voice.

"The tip. The papers say it's missing. Is he eating them?" I asked watching his eyes. From what I had learned so far, the Rakum weren't cannibals, but they were excellent killers. Keifer had not answered or acknowledged my question. He stared far off and when I wiggled in his arms, he grinned and looked down on me.

"Might be," he said and kissed my forehead. "You said now she'll provoke him. Did you give her my idea?"

"Yeah, she's trying it next session. I'll ask her about it when we reconnect."

Keifer had given me a phrase in their language that he felt would prompt the man to reach out to him privately. He wanted to help and he was just plain curious. One thing about the Rakum—they didn't have curiosity before their fall; interest in anything other than blood, sex, and violence was beyond them. But the *mortal* Keifer wanted so much to know everyone's business that I had once teased him for being nosy.

Kiefer moved to sit up. It's Saturday and I planned to take him into the city for a little bumming around. He had never been to the ballet and the Bessemer Arts Council was putting on a performance written by a local celebrity. We showered together and afterward, I made breakfast. We ate at the table where I read the newspaper on my tablet and he played on his phone. Then it was time to go.

Outside, the winter welcomed February as it always did in Alabama—with a lot of freezing rain but rarely any snow. He piloted us into town in his Jeep SUV and we looked around the mall. He doesn't "window shop" but I had learned that about the Rakum. His eyes scan the people and the exits.

In his Rakum days, he'd been a soldier, which means of the brothers in his pack, he was assigned to perform various military tasks. I learned back when I met El-A that their structural system started at the top with the Ten Fathers (ancient men with mysterious roots), and under them were one hundred Elders (each exponentially more powerful than their inferiors, and all haughty assholes, according to the Rakum I've met), and then the remainder of the 100,000 consisted of grunts of various skills and talents. El-A had been his pack's lieutenant, so a soldier. Pitch and Keifer were, too, but there were many other roles to fill. Even though they are human now, I enjoy learning about them from before.

After an enjoyable dinner at a nearby café, we headed to the restored playhouse. Nothing of note happened until we reached the concession stand. I spied a gorgeous woman behind me in the line. She had the look of a super-model, lithe and too tall, with long bones and a willowy stature. She made eye contact and looked away as I did (end of that story). But as it turned out, the man beside her knew my Keifer.

"Kfir, kazak!"[3] he said before launching into a conversation in their language. He was Keifer's height and weight and wore a long-sleeved dress-shirt with the cuffs rolled to mid-forearm. I noted his tanned arms, free of tattoos (most Rakum have them). He was trim in black jeans that touched the floor around heavy workboots. He flicked his gaze to me as I took note of his appearance. When I completed my scan of his curly black hair and handsome face, I offered a polite grin and looked aside.

---

[3] Kazak, "Be strong," the Rakum's multi-use "hello" greeting.

He continued to speak in their language and in the midst of their conversation, Keifer put his arm around me. I returned my attention and the man glanced at me as if their topic had turned to Ruth Angleton. For the millionth time, I wished I understood their language. Rakum Hungarian is guttural, poetic, and dark; I know a handful of words, but that's it.

They spoke another long minute; the man gestured to the model and waved one hand in what looked like a *she's nothing* gesture. One peek at her face and she was looking off into space, her slight hips shifted right and her hands framing her tiny waist. Then I heard the name *Pitch* and I looked at the stranger's face. He smiled with what appeared to be approval.

"What? Do you know him?" I asked and both men chuckled the same way. I looked up and to my right and Keifer grinned down on me, his height always making me feel more feminine than I probably am. "What?"

The stranger looked left and right and pulled his girl's arm in such a way that Keifer guided me to follow. Now out of line for concessions, I hid my irritation and was led to the far wall. No one stood near and Keifer positioned me facing the wall with he and the other Rakum facing the milling crowds. The model stood to the side, her gaze riveted to the chandelier.

"Pitch was our captain in the Old Days," the stranger said and Keifer nodded.

I didn't expect to be introduced as we do in polite (human) society, so I did it myself. "What's your name?"

"Ivan," he answered with a miniscule check on his woman, who still gaped at the high ceilings.

"Okay, Ivan, I'm Ruth. Tell me what's so funny about me treating your former captain?"

"Oh, nothing funny," he countered. "Not funny in the way you mean. In a *human* way." He had whispered the word even though no one was near. "You tell her, K." He turned his eyes to my lover who again draped his arm about my shoulders and kissed my hair.

"I've told you how we all had different tastes and proclivities, right?" he said softly, and I said yes. "Pitch hated mortals and spent his free time giving them hell. Myself, Ivan, many of us liked your kind, appreciated your service and enjoyed your soft places."

The model turned her face to the conversation and spoke to Ivan in a voice that sounded like a crying cat.

"Yowwww-vuhn, less s-s-s-s-eet. Mies feet, Yow-vuhn." She lifted a heel to her buttock (buttock-*area*, it was very flat) and when her fingers grasped the shoe, I noticed they were four inches and spiked.

Ivan ignored her as if she hadn't spoken and he captured my gaze when I diverted from the princess.

"K said you're Pitch's therapist. If he comes back for a third session, watch it."

Ivan looked to Keifer who huffed a small laugh. I looked at his profile, but he didn't look down.

"Pitch might be mortal, but he'll never see you as more than a possible target for his jollies." Ivan then inhaled with an idea and asked Keifer in a low voice, "What's this about tongues?"

Now they were discussing the murders. I strained to understand, but only for a few seconds. I mean, dammit, I was missing concessions. Then Ivan switched to English and my ears perked.

"The tongue talks," he said as if those three words explained the universe.

Keifer inhaled so I listened for his reply, but then he

answered in Rakum. I sighed and looked at the line for popcorn. In another three minutes, the topic changed, evident by their intonation. I widened my eyes listening to the incomprehensible new conversation and it dragged on several more minutes. Finally, I stepped out from under Keifer's arm and went inside to find our seat.

Thirty minutes into the first act, he hadn't joined me so I crept past the row of ballet fans and peeked into the lobby. They were still there. The model had slid down the wall, her narrow ass on the Berber carpet and her eye vacant, fixed on nothing. Keifer and Ivan were speaking close and before I twirled around, I'm pretty damn sure Ivan kissed his mouth. *Tenderly*, like Keifer kisses me. I don't want to go into it right this moment, but the Rakum cleaved to each other in one way or another back in the day. Sometimes that meant sexually. I guess he and Ivan *really* missed each other. Maybe I would tease him about it later tonight in bed, but for now? I'm getting my ballet on.

At intermission, Keifer settled on my right and tucked me under his wing. It wasn't until we were sitting in the Jeep awaiting our turn to exit the parking garage that Keifer spoke.

"Ivan looks good." He peeked my way and then back to the blinkers of the cars in front of us. "That woman though, *shsssss.*"

I grinned. "Yow-ven! Myz feet!" I said in a whine.

"He ought to try a real woman," Keifer added with a wistful headshake.

My thoughts returned to the model's face, body, general shape. Keifer got wind of my dubious reaction.

"You didn't know that was a man?"

I frowned. Being a scientist and extremely attune to details, I had to ponder longer than usual. I prided myself in being able to tell a person's birth gender at a glance. I didn't doubt Kiefer saw it, he'd been alive centuries and could not be fooled by make up and surgery. Finally, I sighed with a half-shrug.

"Well, she looked amazing. Brava," I said with a little clap to the air.

Keifer returned a wry huff. "I guess I don't like the ballet." Keifer hit his turn signal begging for a Good Samaritan among the Bessemer folk.

"Oh? That's too bad," I said looking out the window. "I like it a lot." The psychotherapist inside awoke and I looked at his profile. "In humans, it arouses emotions. Did you pay attention to the music? Did you feel anything odd inside?"

Keifer thought it over and after several long seconds, said no, and offered nothing else.

"Help me understand," I said, and he nodded he would. Since we met, he had been helping me treat his people; knowing what did what to his spirit was my secret. "You were sitting beside me two hours. What did you see and hear in that time?"

I had watched a story play out between two young women in love with a unicorn, which at the end of the show, turned into a handsome prince. He chose the younger of the two sisters because her heart had been pure. The music was sung in Italian, so I did not understand the words, but Keifer would have. Like all Rakum, he spoke multiple languages, Italian among them.

He still hadn't answered, so I backed up my question to before he sat down. "Okay, after Ivan warned me about Pitch and I heard you switch off talking about Patient 7, what was the rest of that about?"

"Church," Keifer said and I wrinkled my nose.

"What church?"

Keifer noted my suspicious tone and he tossed me a kind smile—a human smile. "Ivan started going to a Rakum church. It's based in Tuscaloosa and they stream the feed through the website. He wants me to watch this past weekend's show."

"Sermon," I corrected, and he looked over. "Church is where they give a sermon and sing songs to Jesus." Then I added, "Is it a Jesus church?"

Keifer shrugged. "Must be. The Bankers[1] follow Jesus and they allow the church to stream on our site."

"Excellent deduction, my dear Watson," I said as a joke and he had no reaction. "You going to watch it?"

He nodded and I hid my sigh. I had been born into Catholicism, but when my stepfather took to praying to Saint Peter while prodding me with his fingers, I decided maybe atheism would be a better choice. I hadn't told Keifer about that stuff and I did not say anything more until he maneuvered us into traffic for the main road.

"For science," I said then keeping my tone light, "you came in and sat beside me. Then what? What did you see or hear first?"

Keifer stared straight ahead. "The woman on my right made a whistling noise as she breathed. The conductor hit the music stand eleven times before the first note was played. In the last act, he hit the same spot seven times instead."

I smiled and shook my head. I hadn't noticed any of that. "Is that all?"

"No, the dancer on the far right was crying as she danced."

I asked him how he knew.

"I saw her crying," he said and glanced my way before

returning to the road.

With a slow nod I faced front and processed all he had said. He did not hear the music, the lyrics, or the singing. He didn't see the fluid movement of dance that defied gravity and challenged the human body to the ultimate test of fitness and agility. A nose whistle, the rhythmic clack of bone on steel, and the tears of a girl. I had much to learn. I slipped my phone from my handbag and spoke it all into my voice recorder. At the end, I said, "From now on, Ruth, I want you to imagine that the Rakum come from another planet. They are similar to us but are completely alien."

On my left, Keifer *humphed* nodding his upper body and his outside hand pulled his hair free of its band, his wavy tresses draped over his broad shoulders. Oncoming headlights occasionally illuminated his dark blond highlights and his strong pecs. I imagined him on top of me, looking down, engulfing me with his embrace.

The Alien in My Bed, by Dr. Ruth Angleton.

Before I met the Rakum, I had already had sex countless times, by choice and by force. After college, I entered graduate school, choosing a psychology program. It made sense that if I learned how to heal myself of the sexual abuse I endured from ages seven to seventeen, I would use that to help other victims. But through college, grad school, and even a few months into hanging my shingle, I was still a Rakum Cow. That unhealthy expression prevented me from growing into the "wholly healed" woman I became after they turned human. Then along comes February 2019, I met Keifer. *Fireworks* at our first eye-meet, no shit. I had stumbled upon a Rakum who graduated anger management therapy before we met. He knew how to be thoughtful to a woman's needs. It was a beautiful thing.

"Tomorrow, I will drive to Tuscaloosa and visit the Rakum church."

Keifer had made a statement, not an invitation, and I expected no less. It would take time to teach politeness and being rude was the least of a Rakum's troubles as he assimilated to his new existence. I said it was a good idea and made chit-chat about nothing the rest of the way home.

It's midnight and I'm turning in. Pitch the Terrible is due to come for session three Monday night. Yay.

♦

I had to pee at 3 a.m. That happens when I drink before bedtime, and Kiefer and I did three shots of 360 Double Chocolate Vodka to add a loosey-goosey edge to our lovemaking. I didn't rouse him as I slipped to the bathroom and closed the door, using my phone screen as a light. I had just finished tinkling when my cell vibrated with a new message. The banner read, *Video, Unknown Sender.* I made sure the volume was bottomed out and I hit the link.

Here is where I admit I have a tiny addiction to porn. No, not like I watch it every night for hours. It's on my phone. Snippets, really. Tiny 30-second clips of coitus, usually anything other than binary sex.

My interest in "extra-relational sexual observation," as we call it in the field, started before there was an internet, so I don't see stopping any time soon. And anyway, I don't see it as a negative activity, so it is disingenuous for me to call it an addiction. When I was in therapy, I was taught to think of it as a "healthy expression of a well female". I

25

clung to this label as the new video clip opened.

It showed a fake-rape or maybe a reluctant-sex scene. A beautifully shaped male backside filled the view as he rammed himself into someone bent forward over an industrial-look bathroom sink. The man's trousers were on the floor, still around his ankles and the receiver had been wearing a skirt, which was now hiked to drape over her back. I turned it up a tiny bit and watched.

Unh. Unh. Unh.

I wasn't embarrassed for Kiefer to know, but I had not yet told him I do this. Also, it hadn't occurred to me who might have *sent* me a sex tape. In fact, I've never had one delivered; I find them online myself when I feel chippy. Then, a new noise occurred, the woman was saying stop. Not only that. She said, *"Please stop, please. You'll ruin it."*

He'll ruin it?

The man only thrust harder and I watched on. The tingling probed my middle and worked down. I was going to need to rub it out, but I didn't like the sound of her pleas. It sounded sincere. I like *fake-rape*, not *real*-rape.

Then she began to cry, still taking the abuse without obvious resistance and still asking him to please stop. With three final immense thrusts, he grunted, shivered, backed, and turned to the camera.

SHIT! It was Pitch!

He grinned into the lens and the film ended.

It took only a minute to rub out my orgasm. I hated Pitch, I hated the video, but I'm only human. Now, I feel guilty because his date sounded so pitiful and I was still aroused. I climbed back into bed and Kiefer did not stir. Damn Pitch to hell. He will NOT win.

26

Rakum Devil

Pitch, Session 3, 7pm, Monday
True-Client Software™ **bolds Client's spoken word**
MedVR™ transcripts used to populate dialog, build entry
Loc: My office on 27th Ave

Post-Notes: He's been gone ten minutes. I'm not going to let him win. *Repeat:* Pitch, the Gigantic Asshole Demon Spawn from hell, will not win this battle.

"Over the weekend, I fucked four different women of four different ethnicities. The third was a transsexual with a brand-new vagina. I called him-her-it a confused freak and poked him-her-it extra hard."

Those are the words he spoke as he crossed the threshold and found his seat, again choosing the softer.

Hello, to you, too, Pitch.

I had used Sunday afternoon to study my ever-expanding Rakum therapy model (RTM, Heather and I are calling it). I used what I learned from Keifer after the ballet to plan a new direction and hoped to steer this raucous Rakum, Pitch, toward a saner response pattern.

BUT-

I had a spat with Keifer upon waking. It had been over something not at all related to humans or Rakum, but about laundry. He washed his black t-shirt with my lingerie, and when my best piece was ruined, he couldn't comprehend why I was so upset. At the time, I didn't understand either; it's just a stupid slip, it can be replaced. I shouted and barked the entire hour it took me to get ready for work and I was still seething when I left the house. I discovered on the drive in that I was angry he hadn't considered my clothing important. He didn't care that it was silk, and his t-shirt was made of shit and plastic. See? I was being a hormonal idiot and when I got to work, I forgot to call and apologize. I worked on paperwork until Pitch arrived and I can't forgive myself for sending Keifer off that way this morning.

I nodded my head when Pitch swiveled his face to mine, noticing I hadn't responded and most likely reading everything I was hiding in my countenance. His lips parted and I jumped in first.

"Did you want to sleep with more people and couldn't, or had you planned a sort of one-on-each-corner system to your weekend?"

His eyebrows came up, his smirk only increasing his attractiveness. I smirked, too, and he completed his grin.

"This time, the number four was arbitrary."

I nodded, having prepped myself to pretend I hadn't seen the video he sent. Keeping him unsure in any measure only helped my cause. Also, I didn't want to reveal how pleased I was at his straight answer. If he would only work with me instead of against me, I could help him transform and find peace in his human form. But I can't say any of that aloud—the framework is a skeleton and no patient should see his own bones.

28

"Did you connect with any of your brethren since I saw you last?" I asked, not meaning Keifer, but he jumped on that anyway.

"I had drinks with your boyfriend after our session Friday. I'm sure he told you. Did he punch himself into your body later and ask about me while he worked you over?"

"No, but he mentioned you Saturday morning. He said ya'll spoke about the session, about me." Again, I wanted to hold the reins, so I asked my next question. "Besides Keifer, do you have any other compatible brethren nearby?"

I had learned that they cleave to one another now that they're sad and pitiful. As Rakum, they lived lives of fulfillment, never caring about anything other than the present pleasure. Now, despite each inheriting a fortune, most could not find peace without professional help.

"You've been sleeping with Kfir how long?" he asked tilting his chin to the side. **"It's been a year, right?"**

I nodded. We slept together on Christmas Eve the year before last, so approximately a year.

"He slept with me in October. You went out of town and right there, on top of your queer-ass lavender duvet, he and I played our favorite games two nights in a row."

I swallowed, unable to prevent a gasp of surprise. The thing about Pitch (and every Rakum I've met so far), he doesn't lie about experiences of sex or violence. My mind raced back to Halloween; I had indeed left Keifer in charge of the house, the mail, our cat, for three nights and four days to get away with my Psych Book Club. Yes, it's just what it sounds like—my fellow therapists gathering to get drunk and read erotica to each other in a lake resort.

"To answer your question, Kfir's the only brother for miles," he added then, pretending to tend a hangnail. **"But he and I were always compatible. In battle, in bed, you name it."** He looked up, his eyes suddenly questioning. **"What makes you so special, I wonder?"**

"What do you mean? Special to Keifer?" I managed, although I was pissed at my boyfriend for cheating with the evil malcontent on my couch.

"Yeah."

Pitch got to his feet and as I had chosen to sit before him on the soft chair, I leaned backward, prepared to rise if he came close. But he stood in place, still butted up to the furniture.

"We fucked over and over, and when we got ready to sleep, I asked him to come home with me. Mate-up. Be with me instead of you. Know what he said?"

I didn't dare respond.

"He said he *prefers* you."

Pitch took one small step and stopped again. I scrambled to a standing position and clasped my hands behind me.

"First, he told me it was because you care about his well-being. But I pressed him and he said he prefers sex with you, too. *You. Specifically.*"

Pitch took another tiny step and I made a casual move to stand behind my chair.

"He came into the world in 1808 and bedded thousands of females in that time, but when you lie down beside him, he said he is calm."

Pitch's voice had developed a new timbre I hadn't heard. I pretended not to notice and listened on.

"He said I will never have that calm inside of me until I know a woman or a man in that way—he said,

selflessly, like him and you."

My face softened at the genuine compliment from my lover to this jerk while I was away.

"So, Doc, here's the thing," he said taking a normal stride so he stood opposite my chair and within arm's reach. I did not move away. **"I want you to teach me how to love that way. And if you don't make progress fast, I'll go on to the next Cow-therapist on the list. Deal?"**

One, I doubt Heather would accept him, and two, I'd warn her *not to* anyway. But to best serve my awful client I answered right back, "If you want this, you have to do what I say and answer what I ask. You would have to allow me to lead the sessions my way."

"Up my sessions to three times a week and we'll see," he replied.

My calendar ran past my mind. He was my only Rakum client for the time being, the previous ones all graduated out. To pay the bills (and keep a sound mind) I had two human regulars, both women in their fifties. I saw Pitch Mondays and Fridays and he's the only one I saw at night. If I added Wednesday night to his treatment, I could move that morning patient and come in late. Who sits in my chair Wednesday morning? Bonnie Frond, narcissist personality who thinks her husband is cheating. I caught Pitch's eye and nodded once. I'd move the Frond woman. Maybe she'd quit me, which I wouldn't mind.

"Would you like to start now?" I asked and pointed for the furniture. He turned in a slow manner and dropped back into the couch.

"What's first?" he asked, his eyes narrowed.

I didn't say the word, but I had to teach him about empathy. No one can love another person until they first recognize another being's pain. In answer I said, "I ask a

31

specifically-directed line of questioning that helps you understand human psychology. Want to try one?"

I sounded chipper, but I was play-acting, imagining in the far left of my mind this man and my Keifer making passionate love on my new comforter. One of them screams with pleasure and my cat tears off down the hall, frightened of the sudden noise.

"Go ahead," he said and leaned back to cross one ankle over his knee. When our eyes locked, he licked his lips with purpose and ran his thumb across the round and scooped neck of his soft sweater. He had dark chest hair matching his black waves on top and they poked out at his machinations. **"Give me number one."**

I looked down to my lap. "You see a woman of twenty-one in a parking lot, her tire is flat. She has a jack, but when you walk past, she's having trouble getting the jack unbolted from its carriage. What do you think a mortal male would do then?"

"Huh," Pitch said in an exhale. The corners of his mouth turned down and he looked left thinking. **"Is she a transsexual?"** he asked, and I raised my brow.

"Transgendered?" I clarified, the video popping back to mind. I asked, "Does it matter?"

My mind recalled what Keifer shared regarding gay, straight, and bi according to the Rakum mindset—they didn't live in such boxes. The Rakum were about pleasure, and only after they turned mortal did they individually discover a sexual preference. I realized I had assumed Pitch preferred women because when he spoke of sex, it was with females.

Except when he feels frisky and Kiefer's alone!

"I guess not," Pitch said dismissing the subject.

I still wondered what would make him ask, but this

treatment method required I remain focused. I gave him a helpful prompt.

"First, imagine what the Rakum would do before 11/13. And then, what would the Pitch before meeting me do. And then, what a mortal would do. Only tell me the last one."

Pitch gave a slow nod. **"My brothers and I watched movies and television to figure this shit out. We could pretend to be friendly until it was safe to do our thing."** He licked his lips and exhaled. **"A mortal man would offer to help. Perhaps, he'd move in and take over, making her stand aside as he changed the tire. Then he'd fasten the jack into place and make sure she was ready to hit the road."**

I was impressed and showed it with my responses, jotting notes with a satisfied nod.

"The next one is similar. That scenario we just discussed is at night, the store is closed and the parking lot empty, save her car and yours. There is one streetlight and it is over her car, but as you can imagine, the remainder of the huge lot is dark. If you were that woman, how would you feel seeing Pitch walk up?"

He thought longer this time, scratched his beard and rubbed his eyes. **"Rabbits are afraid of wolves."**

At his statement, I looked up from my notes. The word "rabbit" has a special meaning to Rakum and I couldn't tell which he meant.

"She probably feels like a rabbit when a wolf walks up. Her heart races and she wonders if she should run. And if she runs, could she be faster than the wolf?"

I nodded. "That's right. That's really good. Wow."

I was surprised to have him answer correctly. My

33

model indicated I'd need to ask seven questions before he would be able to get inside another's mindset. I made notes on the pad in my lap, smiling and planning the next question. I didn't notice Pitch changing position, his movement so stealthy that I continued until I was done. I poked a period at the end of my last sentence and raised my gaze, my pencil touching the pad. Pitch had scooted to the edge of his chair, leaning over, his forearms resting atop is thighs, his face tilted degrees to the right, his eyes waiting for mine to connect. When they locked, my blood ran cold.

"Ruthy, Ruthy, I got a sweet toothy," the Rakum sang, his voice a mixture of guttural and silk. *"Sit on my lap and you'll hear the whole truthy. Daddy has a toothy for his sweet little Ruthy."*

I couldn't move.

How…?

Who…?

Pitch held my eye, his hands had been dangling, but he opened them palms out. His fingers fluttered, inviting me to come close. To climb into his lap. To help him with that huge sweet tooth Daddy carried in his pants.

This man is a monster.

A monster I invited in, that I invited to help, and that I thought wanted my help.

My eyes sprang tears of their own accord and I stood on shaky knees. I'm not a child and my father is dead. My stepfather, too. The youth pastor who raped me in the choir closet is alive, but he's in Orlando or some shithole sticking his business into someone else's child.

Pitch had not changed position and appeared to be awaiting my answer. How did he know what my dad used to say to me when he came home drunk and mom went to bed early, sleeping under the influence of too many

34

Valium? I pointed to the exit, but my voice did not work. There are two people in the world besides myself who knew *Daddy's Sweet Tooth Ruth* song: my dead father and my psychotherapist, Jenny. Jenny would never share that information. How did he...

"My cock isn't as big as Daddy's." The pointer finger of one hand mimicked an erection standing tall. **"You'll like it. Come on. Let me show you I can love you better than he did. Better than Roberto. Better than Aaron the Closet Pervert."**

He knows everything!

I commanded low and clear for him to leave and inside, my mind raced to Jenny's office to inspect the security of her filing system.

Pitch stood and stepped to the door. **"I'm going to have you, Doc. It's only a matter of time. And Kfir won't stand in my way. See, the blood between us is thicker than a flimsy loyalty to a Cow with a fat ass and aging face."**

I'd like to end this journaling session with a great bang, how I shouted at him and scared him away with my semi-automatic .9mm. But I didn't. I waited for him to give up staring. He eventually wandered out and when I played tonight's voice recording, I timed that silence. From his last word to the elevator door ding, seven minutes elapsed. I had stood staring at his demon's face seven whole minutes before he slithered out.

I'm taking tomorrow off, and I'll find out how he got hold of Jenny's files. I will also find out where Keifer's head is in all this. If Pitch is correct and my Rakum boyfriend would choose his brother over me, I need to break it off.

But Pitch DOES NOT WIN. Wednesday at 7pm, I'll see him for session #4. This bitch is tougher than she looks.

The Doctor's Files

eifer didn't come home last night. I got in from that hellish session with his demonic brother and the apartment sat empty. My first thought when I entered, closed and locked the door behind me, and crossed into the living room was that he had gone for good. A preternatural void filled the place and I stepped to the bedroom to see if he'd taken his clothing. After finding everything in place, including his toothbrush and floss, I allowed myself to shower and go to bed.

When I awoke, he hadn't come home. There are no messages on my phone nor any emails explaining where he might be. If he was a normal mortal man, I'd be concerned, but he's not. I remind myself that for two hundred years, he fulfilled himself in any way he desired and his only restrictions came from brethren with his very same interests in blood, sex, and violence. I saw plenty of all three growing up, but my worst experience didn't come close to his old favorites.

"I missed you last night. See you soon," I sent to Keifer's phone and forced myself to let that be it. We made a commitment and hadn't slept apart, except for that one

ladies' retreat. I asked him not to sleep with other women. It didn't occur to me that I should specify not to sleep with men. *Check.* Learned another new thing about the Rakum. Thanks, Keifer.

It's ten and Jenny has lunch at eleven. I texted her that I was coming and she returned a thumb's up. Time to face the music and possibly have to think about the monsters from my past. Ironic that I lived with and was accosted by monsters my whole life and now, as an adult, I managed to invite the worst one of all right into my office. Great job, Ruth.

In the foyer, I hefted my purse to my shoulder, the weight of my gun giving me comfort. I bought it in college for self-protection after a girl in my dorm was attacked on her way to the library. I had taken one two-hour lesson and was afterward distracted by life. I carry it now, but I don't clean it and I never practice shooting. I assume it will fire if I need it, but to be honest, I never expect it to come out of my purse. What was the old saying? *Carry gun, never shoot. Go unarmed, lose your loot.*

I shook my head at my rambling thoughts and headed to the car. The drive to Jenny's would take thirty minutes, so to fill the silence, I dialed into the BMH chatroom. My car will read it to me, but there were no new posts to my thread with Heather. It had been six days since we chatted, which means she would have had her follow-up with Patient 7. Part of my mind wondered why she hadn't checked in, but then I pictured Pitch's horrid expression when leaving my office, and Heather's Patient 7 moved to the back of my mind.

I clicked on the XM Radio comedy channel, hoping for a little distraction. It worked. One guy had me laughing so hard that I took a photo of the radio screen to research his deets later. By the time the sets grew boring with newer, lamer talent, I had arrived at Jenny's.

Unlike myself, she runs her office at home. I'd never allow my patients to know where I live, but she told me she's safe with her German Shepherd and shotgun. The office is built atop her garage, so I scaled the staircase and let myself in. Jenny's voice trickled from an interior consultation room and I leaned against the back of a lobby couch she had picked up, by the look of it, at Macy's.

Jenny did not know about the Rakum; I tactfully avoided the topic during my treatment. Why share a supernatural thing with someone who would never know it as I did? The Rakum were human these days and I long decided that I would never speak of it to anyone not already aware of them.

Jenny's practice was exclusive to sexually marginalized clients, men, women, and transgendered, who struggle with interpersonal relationships and/or society at large. By the time the wall clock clicked eleven, my friend and confidante walked her patient past me and waved him out the door. When I was at my lowest, I'd seen Jenny for anxiety and depression. She brought me back from the edge, taught me coping skills, and when I had graduated college and held my license in hand, she allowed me to intern under her for two years. That had been six years ago and since then, our visits are social, not clinical.

Jenny whipped around in a dramatic twirl and opened her arms. "Ruth! Come here!" she belted, grabbing me into a hug. She squeezed me to her chest and her boobs seemed too firm. I leaned out of the hug and looked down. She giggled and grabbed my right hand. "What do you think?" she asked and turned my palm to conform to her left breast. "Little present to myself. Feels natural, right?"

Without making contact with her nipple, as her brassiere was extremely thin, I cupped the flesh and moved an inch both ways. I looked into her face with sorrowful eyes. "Sugar, are they still healing? I mean, it's really hard."

Jenny replaced my hand with her own and studied the roundness with a thoughtful gaze. "No, it's not. What do you mean? It's great."

I put my hand to my own breast. I was correct. Mine was very pliable and soft. Hers? No mush. Jenny's smile evaporated and she moved her open palm to my breast, first the left and then right. Unlike my carefulness, her thumbs brushed my nipples on both sides, and without a care, she fondled them several times, jerking her hand to her bra and back again, comparing back and forth. On her fourth pass, I was grinning, my nipples hard and sending signals to my lower body. I pushed away her fingers and covered my bosom with one forearm.

"Buy me a drink first, doc," I said in a film noir accent. "I'm not that kind of girl."

"That mother-effing-quack-Osco!" she yelped and shot past me to her interior office. I followed and she plopped behind her desk and picked up the landline. "Sit tight, Ruth. Be right with you."

I gave her the go-ahead nod and sat across from her desk, in an absent manner comparing it to mine. She barked at Dr. Osco's receptionist and slammed down the handset. With an exhale to calm her expression, Jenny fanned her palms onto the desktop and met my eye.

"He'll call me back," she said, her tone even. "So!" Jenny then clapped once and leaned back, propping both low-heel-shoed feet onto the shiny pine desktop. "What's up? How you doin' these days? How's Keifer? Saw your online check-in from the FunRun. He's hot enough to melt

39

butter."

I smiled in a huge nod that included my upper body. "He is, and trust me, it doesn't cool down. It's been a year now and he still melts me through and through."

Keifer and I kept pace with the top fifteen runners that day, although I suspect he could have won it. One of the things he told me when we first met was his psychotherapist encouraged him to "fail a little." That it would help him one, feel more human, and two, *appear* more human. I can't decide if I should add this to my Rakum model; I'm still on the fence about encouraging any living being to fail on purpose.

"You look fantastic," Jenny said scoping me from where she sat, her approving nod included. A self-proclaimed bisexual in a monogamous lesbian relationship, Jenny possessed a self-actualized, hypersexual personality and did not censor opinions.

I shrugged with a small grin. "That's what they tell me." I had always been shapely, bordering on chubby, which must be perfect since the males around me always wanted a piece. Growing up, I hated my body, considered it a traitor constantly getting me into all sorts of trouble. But at twenty, I was hostessing at a Frog Shack when a co-worker recommended Jenny. She taught me to love myself, and I infinitely cherish her affection and professionalism.

Twelve months of talk therapy and she graduated me out. She also lettered for me to enter the PhD program at her alma mater. Check this—when I received my degree, it was Jenny and her wife Tiff representing my family in the audience.

"Ruth, my sweet, I can't imagine why you wanted to see me like this." She looked around the room, decorated as if soon to be photographed by *Psychology Today*. With a cheeky grin, she pointed to her watchless wrist. "I have another patient in forty-one minutes."

I sighed and she turned serious. "I needed to ask you something. Last night, a new patient revealed that he had read my files—the ones from your office. I needed to know if you had a security breach."

Jenny's eyes grew huge and she jerked her feet to the floor. Showing me a wait gesture, she stepped to a wall of three tidy wood-laminate filing cabinets. Jenny did not digitize her sessions, never had, using only tape and film with a single copy locked down. She pressed the thumb-lock on each cabinet in succession and they were sealed. Then, she showed me the same wait finger and reached for her landline.

"Pumpkin," she said after a moment, "can you come up here?"

I watched her face and wondered what Tiff might add. Jenny's behavior gave me enough reason to think maybe she had experienced some sort of problem with her files. She hung up and sighed.

"I had a receptionist. I had to fire her." Jenny cursed to the side, using *dang* instead of *damn*.

"Was she fired for mishandling files?" I asked and heard Tiffany scaling the outside steps.

Jenny shook her head. "No, Tiff caught her leaving work early. Sneaking out. Leaving the place un-manned when I was paying her to man it."

"What's up?" Tiffany said, her tone serious. Thick, strongly-built, and blond, Tiffany Speakman had played professional softball until an injury sidelined her to coach. Now she took the community college intramural team to task. She flicked her chin. "Hey, Root. You good?"

"Ruth thinks someone got into her file. Could that

little witch have something to do with that?" Jenny asked stepping close to peck Tiff's cheek.

"Geez, I hope not," she replied and looked upward in thought. "Come to think of it, she left the cabinets unlocked the night I found the place abandoned." Tiffany looked at me to add, "Door unlocked, lights on, left us wide open. I told Jen to fire her, the little brat."

"I'll run it down, Ruth. Are you okay?" Jenny leaned against the threshold now that we stood in the waiting room area. She automatically assumed whomever spouted my past stirred a stick in my old wounds. I guess that is as good a description as any, come to think of it.

I exhaled, prepared to share a little and get a little help in return. "Keifer has a friend from his past that needed anger management. That's sort of my specialty the past twelve months so I took him on. In last night's session, he quoted back to me what I've only told one other soul in the world." I pointed a finger-gun to Jenny.

"I'm sorry if it was here, hon, that you got outed," Tiff said, backing for the door.

The confidentiality of my files steered her away without me even asking. I thanked her and when Jenny and I were alone, she motioned that we re-enter her office.

"This friend of Keifer's," she said finding a seat in a patient choice, not her desk chair. Set up much like mine with different types of chairs to choose from, I sat in the one matching hers and facing her three-quarters.

"Let's call him Dick," I replied, and my smirk said it all. "He's a horrid narcissistic sociopathic personality and every time I see him, I want to run the other way. But—"

"An equal part wants to help him and see it through," Jenny finished in my stead.

She knew me very well. I inhaled to add more and my

phone chimed. The screen displayed Pitch's contact and my gaze met Jenny's, who revealed normal curiosity. I hit the off button, pretending it was nothing. I didn't want to know if he was sending me a text or a new video, but either way, Jenny didn't need to know about it. First things first.

"He wants to keep me off balance," I told her. "The more idiotic he can make me appear, the smarter *he* looks."

"Typical," Jenny said with a nod. "Rest assured, I will investigate and prosecute anything I can on this breach, but until then, let me give you some weapons against any future provocations, okay?"

I exhaled with relief; this is exactly what I needed. Then, in a thoughtful, non-hurried manner (despite the fact that she had a patient coming in 36 minutes), Jenny counseled me as an equal and with full knowledge of my horrific abusive history. By the time the lobby door buzzed, we were hugging it out. She handed me a folded sheet of paper.

"Don't read that here. I just wanted you to see it. This woman was one of my patients. Just keep her family in your thoughts, okay?"

I read the pain in her eyes, recalling two weeks ago she'd told me that one of her patients was found murdered in her home in downtown Birmingham. Now, another one? My mind went to Patient 7, but behind me, Jenny's next client cleared his throat. After a polite goodbye, I went to my car. I'd be ready for that asshole Pitch in tomorrow's session. He won't be able to surprise me again.

Once sitting in my car, I texted Keifer with, *"Thinking about you,"* and a heart emoji. Then I unfolded the paper. Jenny had printed out a page from an internet newspaper. It was Patient 7 and I didn't like where the clues were headed.

emil jersey

TRANS WOMAN MURDERED, FBI TAKES CASE

CORINTH, MS (WKRP) — The family of a trans-woman who was raped, killed, and disfigured in Corinth this week is seeking answers.

24-year-old Loretta Fineburg was a hardworking secretary for one of the city's largest law firms, attending night classes to one day pass the Bar.

An activist for the local LGBTQ+ community and born a male, Loretta completed her transformation two years ago. Living as female, "she was finally happy in her own skin," her parents told WKRP's James Ullman.

"She had one goal," her father told WKRP, "to make sure everyone around her was smiling. Her whole existence was to make people laugh. Who could hurt such an angel?"

Police say Fineburg didn't show up for work Monday, which sent friends to her apartment in the eastside. There, she was found deceased. Authorities confirm her tongue had been severed. The third such murder puts the case in the hands of the FBI, according to sources, and is now considered a serial killing...

Roof-roof-roof," my step-father Roberto yipped on hands and knees as he approached my bed and swooped close to lick my nose with his fat tongue. He was too fast and got me again across my cheek. I was tangled in my blankets and tried to shuffle out, but he used his paws

44

to yank me free of the bed. "Roof," he said again and used his teeth to nip my nightshirt. Then I noticed he had set his video camera near the bed. My skin broke out in terrified bumps. I begged him to let me go to the bathroom. I thought maybe I could lock myself in, make a plan, but he was pulling me to the floor to play doggies on the carpet...

The Church

Wednesday morning, the nightmare disappeared by the time I brushed my teeth. I blew off my pre-noon patient and rescheduled her for Friday. That'll make Friday suck, but there was no going this morning.

I'm dreading my session with Pitch. I didn't cancel him. He can't win. After all I've survived and conquered, I will NOT LET HIM WIN. I don't care what he used to be. I'm more man than he is. More *hu-man*, I mean.

I had taken a bite of a tomato sandwich when I heard the front door open. I hadn't seen Keifer since Sunday morning and I wiped the corners of my mouth, swallowed, and primped my hair before heading out of the kitchen nook. Keifer dropped his keys into the ceramic bowl at the foyer side-table and looked up when I popped in my head.

"Hey," he said and took extra time to dig through his pockets seeking something else.

"Hey," I replied and walked toward him. Should I kiss him? Pat his arm? Hug? I hoped when I got close, he'd initiate one of those so I might reciprocate. He was still fishing his pockets, pulling out coins, a pen, and a marble. I grinned. Where did he get a marble? Then he huffed and held open his palm.

"Guess what this is."

I got closer to look upon his object, my relaxed-fit Victoria Secret Tee brushing his fingers. He did not attempt any of my greeting options, so I didn't either.

"What's that? A bullet?" I asked and reached for the item. It was round and rusty, and once in my fingers, it had weight as if made of lead.

"Musket ball. Found it at the battlefield." He took the item back and dropped it into his pocket.

The battlefield is an hour away; we went there together last summer and learned about the local Civil War skirmishes. And it was west, not north; in Lowndesboro, not Tuscaloosa. My lover had been driving again and I gave him a break. As I mentioned, he needed mental stimulation, and a lot of it.

I made a noise of interest and looked at his profile, his eyes on the accumulated mail. He was freshly showered, smelled of aftershave and soap, and his long brown hair was loose and fluttering in the air from the ceiling vent. He had been gone more than 36 hours, no word, no text, no call. A Rakum wouldn't care, but he was mortal now. I watched his perfect fingers slide across the various envelopes and planned my next words. They had to be right.

"I missed you," I said and as his face was coming up to mine, I added, "I went up to visit Jenny. She says hi."

Keifer grinned when our eyes met and I hated how my nervous system reacted. I released my breath as my brain fuzzed, the desire to feel his touch blossoming more quickly than I could stop it. I don't only love him for sex; why can't my body understand that?

"I think you're asking me where I've been," he said, his grin tucking into his cheek. His beard was thicker, as if he hadn't shaved since Saturday. "Doc, what do I say

47

next?" he asked, lowering his chin to appear comical and inquisitive altogether.

I forced a smile. "Yes, because we have a committed romantic relationship, you and I would announce whenever we have to be apart for an evening or more. If ever we are surprised by a reason to leave, we would call or at least text the other." I delivered my teaching in a forensic manner and he nodded.

"And if I was in a place you wouldn't like me to be? A place I might not want to admit I was sleeping?" he asked and I had the sense he was baiting me, provoking me in the way of the Rakum.

My Rakum "master" *(Cringe!)* did that on a consistent basis, intentionally pushing my buttons to get a reaction. Keifer, as a rule, was polite and generous of spirit, so I was surprised to suddenly be comparing him to El-A.

El-A had been as handsome as Keifer, Pitch, any number of Rakum I've laid eyes on. It's something about the way they're made, they're simply appealing. Different sizes, ethnicities, and personalities, but before and after their transition, each one enthralls with his allure.

El-A was Latino, and I never heard another name for him. I had escaped my last abuser by leaving Florida. I came here, drank too much, and worked anywhere I could find a job. I had a high school degree so I enrolled in night classes and found an apartment I could afford. One evening, on my 19th birthday, I was drinking (yes, illegally, sorry-not-sorry) with a coworker at a downtown pub. Someone poked my back and I turned. The way I remember it, a beautiful Mexican, tall, strong, with skin smooth and brown, and hair so black it reflected a crazy shine, asked me to move aside. The barkeep was handing him two beers and I leaned away, but my mind had left my

48

body. Looking into El-A's eyes caused a fugue, and even as I could not move or speak in that moment, I recognized that he knew what was happening. A knowing smile crossed his face and he put out his hand.

"Come with me, señorita," he had said, his voice flowing like honey into my ears. "I have what you need."

And I went off with him.

My past disappeared for the weeks El-A held me close. He treated me to dinner, dancing, movies, drinking, partying, and lots and lots of sex—at first with him alone, but as the nights passed, his friends (later introduced as his brethren) were invited. All of us at once, and sometimes I was the only female on board. None of that phased them, and everyone was sure to be satisfied in some way before sunup.

During these crazy three weeks, I learned about the Rakum. I learned I was a "Cow," a mortal supernaturally drawn to them, and that I *belonged* to El-A. He told me that my blood belonged to him, but my body was for them all. Then came his only rule for me—no sex with mortals. *Ever.* I had no problem with that, as mortal men had been abusing me since first grade. Over time, I shared my past and he put a guard on me. For the rest of my life as a Rakum Cow, a highly trained bodyguard, male and a eunuch, was on my tail 24/7.

After thirty nights in his bed, El-A found a new girl and he moved me into an apartment he owned in Hoover (fifteen miles south of where I live now). He paid my bills, even my college tuition, and came by for sex and blood every eight weeks. My bodyguard kept males from approaching or hurting me, so I hadn't a complaint. In 2012, he stopped coming around and I learned down the road that something had happened to their leaders. But his lawyer had pre-paid for my tuition which was huge back then.

My trip down memory lane showed on my face, for Keifer smiled wider and put a warm palm to my cheek.

"I was at church," he said and pulled me close to touch his lips to my forehead. When he pulled back, he held my gaze.

"For two nights?" I asked, aware of how I sounded. Keifer's eyebrows went up and I read he was working to remember the correct mortal response. My female support personality kicked in and I answered for him. "It's in Tuscaloosa? Is that what you said?"

Keifer nodded. "They built a church that looks like a tomb. Here, I took some pictures."

He searched his phone and inside, I was thrilled, and I put aside my suspicions. My Rakum-now-mortal lover is eighty miles away among his own kind and thinks, "I wonder if Ruth would be interested in seeing this. Let me take some photos in case…" That thought would hold me a long time and I was grinning as he handed over his cell.

"Whoa," I said by reflex and zoomed the first picture.

The structure was a perfect cube. It had smooth, steel-gray walls with no windows, and double front doors of frosted glass. In contrast, the landscaping was lavish with winterproof flora in the bordered beds, and carefully trimmed boxwoods framed the building.

Keifer swiped to the next photograph. This one was inside, as if stepping past the threshold and looking straight in. At the far wall, a bema and podium sat center, and there were no pews, no wall hangings, and no icons. I grinned at him, a zillion questions on my tongue. He smiled back and swiped the next photo.

"David, Foin, Jarett, and Rusp," he said pointing to

the men all glancing to the camera as if he had said, *cheese!*
"And you met Ivan."

Each guy was handsome in his own way and I
recognized the man from the theater standing in the center.
He had his hand on the one named David's shoulder as if
they had been chatting when the shutter snapped. When
he swiped one more time, the photo showed Ivan flipping
a bird to the camera and Keifer switched the photo in a
jerk. I grinned.

"Are you embarrassed?" I asked with humor and
curiosity. My normally stoic lover made that photo
disappear as if I shouldn't see it.

He glanced at my face once before giving a very
human sigh and calling it up again. Ivan's right hand shot
the photographer a bird. So what? Then I saw it, the one
called Jarret was behind him, almost invisible in shadow,
and he had shoved both hands down the front of Ivan's
jeans. I still didn't get why Keifer was shy about the photo.
I looked at his face for an explanation and he gave me a
little-boy grin.

"Just trying to be polite. Be a mortal. How did I do?"

His tone was slightly disingenuous, but I let it go. I
mean, he used to be a monster. I think a little handball in
the church foyer is allowed. He kissed my forehead and
swiped to a new photo.

"And here is what it looks like when they get
underway."

"Wow," I whispered, studying the photo and again
reverse-pinching to zoom and look more closely at the
attendees. Forty or so men stood with their backs to the
camera, all facing the front, listening to the one called
David who stood at the podium, his mouth open, looking
over the group. "Only Rakum come to the service? Is it

like a private club? Is that how you keep mortals away?"

Keifer nodded. "David owns the property and it's fenced much like a mortal country club. If anyone wants to come in, they would need clearance and the gate man only allows in folks who speak our language."

"Eventually, a human is going to learn that language," I said not meaning anything by it, but Keifer stiffened and gently removed his phone from my hand.

"That is impossible," he said and pocketed the phone.

I looked at him with wide eyes, surprised at his indignant tone. "Oh? I didn't mean any offense."

I had learned a few phrases when with El-A, but it would do no good to mention that now. He said nothing more and it occurred to me that perhaps he wasn't so sure. I switched the topic.

"Did you know David before? Does he consider himself a preacher?"

The man who founded the Rakum church was younger than Keifer, appeared barely twenty-five, with reddish-brown hair, freckles, bright eyes—possibly green—and a friendly smile. He looked to me like a choir boy and it was extremely difficult to imagine him murdering anyone in cold blood, which every Rakum I ever met said they did with glee in the Old Days.

Keifer turned to leave the foyer. "As far as I can tell, he's just David. He has a few of the brethren helping him when we break out into smaller groups to talk. Ivan's one of the leaders."

I followed him to the kitchen and when he rifled through the fridge, I reached past him and grabbed sandwich fixings to make him a meal.

"So, you liked it? You went back the next day? You stayed over? Is there a place to sleep? Or did you stay at

Ivan's?" Of all the brothers, he said Ivan's name the most often.

Keifer smiled at my question barrage and watched me prepare his food. He leaned on the smooth granite counter, kicking his long legs out to cross his ankles. I looked at his body in the way I always did and he flexed his pecs for me as he answered.

"Ivan said the mortals call it fellowship," he said with a curious faraway look. "After David spoke to us a while about God and what He expects from us, we split into groups and talked about whatever came to mind. It was very informal. I had assumed it would be a dark, fake, and unhappy place, but I felt at home. I felt good." He met my eyes. "I felt really good, actually."

I returned his smile. "It sounds like you believe in God now." I didn't mean to say those words and as they left my mouth, a sense of dread pierced me to the core. I had vowed to never date or even cohabitate with a Christian, male or female, and hadn't since leaving my abusers. Now my heart sank as Keifer's grin widened and a light appeared in his face that hadn't been there before.

"Yeah, I do. I confessed." He reached for the sandwich I had completed on autopilot. "When Ivan finished telling me how he met Jesus, I thought, hell, why don't I meet Him, too? Ivan made it sound like I'd know instantly if He was real, that all I had to do was open my mind to Him, focus on Him in the same way I used to focus my heart and mind on my brethren to read them in the Old Days. So, I did."

Keifer bit into his lunch, squirting mayonnaise and tomato pieces onto his napkin. I had pasted on a passable "good for you" face and so far, he bought it.

"Have you spoken to Jesus?" he asked, his eyes as

serious as I've ever seen them. I shook my head. "You should try it. I'm not shitting you."

Still speechless, my fake face nodded. Keifer's shined brighter than before as he continued.

"When I finished saying those words, my entire body filled with the most amazing sensation. I was whole. *Complete.*" Keifer shook his head. "Ivan said that because our relationship with our Rakum Fathers was spiritual, it is easy for us to hear the Maker."

I said nothing and maybe my fake-face lost its structure. Keifer's smile melted into concern.

"Are you okay?" he asked and after wiping a napkin to his chin, he touched my shoulder.

"Yes, I'm just, wow!" I said in an attempt to recover. My phone chirped the hour in my purse and I had my out. "Oh, geesh, I have to go." I grabbed Keifer into a hug and tiptoed up to kiss his neck. "I have some accounting paperwork and then Pitch at seven. I'll be home after that."

"How did it go Monday night?" he asked, holding me in place as I tried to squirm free. "Did he behave?"

"Sure," I lied and kissed his mouth to keep moving. "He's a royal asshole, but we'll get there."

He released me and watched me gather my plate to drop in the sink. He followed me to the door and I patted my hair in the mirror, my back to him. He was studying me, I'm sure, reading my deceit. I needed time to process his big news. *I need time. Time. Time.* I needed to nip it in the bud with a little redirection.

"To be honest, he scared me a little," I said and only glanced his way once before putting my hand to the knob. "But I promise, everything is fine. He answered my empathy questions perfectly. He's getting it."

Keifer didn't buy it, but he let me leave. I felt his eyes

on my back as I closed the door and scooted to the elevator.

Keifer's a goddamn Christian?

I could not wrap my mind around it, and I didn't want to. In the car, my finger hovered over Jenny's number. She knew my dislike of religion and religious people. But… She'd be with clients. Then my phone dinged with a message from Keifer's cell.

"I'm returning to Tuscaloosa. See you in a few days. How's that? I let you know." (smile emoji)

With a huff, I focused on the road and stored up my anger against the One trying to steal Keifer away.

The Disciple

Because of the way I rushed out of my lover's presence, I reached my office early. I sat in my desk chair and stared at the oscillating screen savers preloaded into my desktop.

Keifer believes in Jesus…

Keifer believes in Jesus?

That statement barely made sense no matter which word I attached an inflection. I rolled it around a few more times, working my doctor hat into position. I didn't have to hate all Christians simply because of events of my past. Since when did a scientist allow an individual's actions to represent an entire subset?

Keifer is a Christian… And he asked me if I've spoken to Jesus.

Wow.

I exhaled and lifted my eyes to the office door. I used to talk to God all the time as a child and I didn't blame Him when my abusers made me cry. Without bringing up the incidents in question, I recalled how *young me* used to curl into a ball after a "play session" with Dad (and later, stepdad) and *young me* would talk to the Jesus on the wall.

He had the kindest eyes…

It was a widely-dispersed Catholic rendering of the Lord Jesus, his head tilted to the side, gazing into the viewers' eyes with an expression that says, "Tell Me what's wrong. I'll help if I can…"

That memory made me smile. And He did help, He really did. Back then I spoke to the Jesus painting as if he was a friend, not like Mom spoke to the priests, but more natural. I'd say, "I'm scared, Jesus. Will You help me go to sleep?"

I'm sitting in my office waiting for that nasty Pitch and remembering, Jesus always helped me fall asleep.

Doesn't this mean I believe in Jesus, too?

Maybe, but I wasn't a Christian, and I was disturbed at the thought of my boyfriend glomming onto God. It was too much to process and I would look inward later—right now, it's time for you-know-who.

Pitch, Session 4, 7:00pm, Wednesday
True-Client Software™ **bolds Client's spoken word**
MedVR™ transcripts used to populate dialog, build entry
Loc: My office on 27th Ave

Notes: None. I'm exhausted. I hope this goes well.

"We're still friends?" he asked when he crossed the threshold and I gestured for a chair. He clucked with a sideways grin. **"Well, well. So now it's The Maker, Kfir, and Ruth sittin' in a tree."** He closed the door behind him with drama and met my eye. **"Is that how the little ditty goes?"**

I forced a grin and waited to see where he'd plant. He chose his same chair and leaned back to cross his ankles. He wore black jeans tonight with a pastel yellow long-sleeved dress shirt, that of course, showcased his dark good looks. When he was sure my eye had reached his chest, he unbuttoned the second and third buttons before settling his arms on the chair rests. I suppose he wanted me to notice his chest hair, and I did. It peeked out much like a pit bull on a leash, giving me the sense it would be beautiful to behold. Pitch was so accustomed to being ogled, that he did not tease me back but waited for me to make the next verbal contribution.

"Does that greeting mean you've spoken to Keifer?" I asked and situated myself at my desk. Tonight, being close and easy to read seemed less important. Five feet of wood between us I desired.

"That's some wild shit, huh?" he said, his tone eerily altruistic. His eye, also, was softer. I remained skeptical as he continued with, **"I never met David Walker, but I know Ivan. I guess it won't be long before your boyfriend moves out."**

"What makes you say that?" I asked, telling myself this was part of his treatment, digging into his interpersonal skillset.

Pitch tipped his head to the side, his lips parted. **"Didn't you read the Rabbit book?"**[2]

I hadn't heard of whatever he meant and my face showed it.

"Oh, doll-face," he said and sat upright to scroll through his phone.

I was surprised at the endearment, but I know he

doesn't mean it the way a woman would enjoy. Still, it doesn't hurt the ears when he looked so very beautiful.

Ruth, geez!

"Right here."

Pitch held out his cell. It was a new model of the brand I use, and he had it protected with a shiny black cover. He hadn't stood to hand me the phone, so I came from around my desk, his behavior different enough that I felt inclined to cut him some slack. Keeping a neutral expression, I stepped closer to take the phone. Pitch turned his hand at the last second, so I ended up half-grabbing his four fingers before my grip secured the device. He wanted that to happen, for us to touch, and I refused to look at his face. I took the device and stepped backward to my desk to sit against the edge.

"*The Rabbit,* by Beth Rider-Stone,"[3] I read off the screen. Nothing about the cover revealed it might be about a Rakum Rabbit, which I am aware of, so I scrolled to the description. *"Beth Rider must die,"* I read and looked at the cover again. *"Bestselling author Beth Rider stumbled upon a hidden and ancient race of vampiric beings… the message in her novels shakes their leaders to the core…"*

"Beth Rider must die…" Pitch said in an eerie horror movie voice. When I braved to meet his eye, he nodded with a grin.

Wait.

A human grin.

"Is this book…?" I did not want to use up our time figuring out some fiction novel. Maybe he would fill in the blanks and save me the time.

"Read it tonight," he said then and stood, presumably to retrieve his phone. **"Kfir's a late bloomer, but the religion he's chasing is the one that destroyed**

our people."

Pitch paced to within four feet, his hand patiently awaiting his cell. Up close, a sensation flashed across my frame. My head, throat, chest, and down to my stomach, and as the iPhone changed possession, he looked me in the eye to speak and heat blossomed lower than before. I'm stove up and shit, my body has no prejudice against the asshole inside my gorgeous Rakum patient.

"If he's fallen in love with the Maker, he won't be able to stay with you and me. The book spells it out." Pitch spoke his piece still close, his eyes flitting from my gaze to my lips and back. I didn't like him, but my flesh began to sing his praises.

I rolled in my lips with a tiny nod, begging internally for him to return to his seat. After another moment, he did, spun on one heel and plopped back down. Stiffly, I circumvented my desktop and sat as well.

"You seem different," I told him. "Does your demeanor have something to do with what Keifer is going through, or maybe something happened since I last saw you that gave you a new perspective?"

Pitch grinned and looked at his hands.

That mortal grin again. His face literally seemed brighter with that mouth. Brighter and younger…

"I haven't analyzed it, but I feel different after our last session." He took a deep breath and exhaled. **"I want to flip the script. I want to woo you."**

Pfffft. Inside, my walls of protection rose to the utmost. While as a rule, Rakum do not *lie,* they do twist fact for their own purposes. This man, filled to the brim with ill-will, was not stating he wanted to court me. No, he said precisely what he meant—woo, draw, manipulate. I listened with a flat expression; I'd been manipulated my entire life and I wouldn't let it happen again.

"I had wanted to maybe do a session or two, see what sort of therapy my sad little brethren have been seeking, and then I was going to take you in this office. But..." Pitch shrugged and gave me that new smile. **"I'm flipping the script."**

I wanted to be speechless, but I'm the doctor. "I don't date patients. You know that, right?" And then I added, "I have a boyfriend, anyway."

"Also, I lied before," he said as if I hadn't spoken. **"I've been attracted to you since Kfir showed me your website. You're my type, strong, sexy, not too tall, not too skinny. And your ass, I'd like to grab it right now."**

"Pitch," I said and did not care for the waver in my tone, "None of that is appropriate."

"As a mortal or as a patient?"

"Both," I answered.

In a smooth movement, Pitch reached into his front jeans pocket and removed a folded sheet of paper which he stood to pass over.

"This letter is to testify that I visited Dr. RL Angleton as a personal research project and as a joke; never did I believe or consider myself her patient or consider her my doctor/therapist. If the doctor has files of our time together, they are not to be considered medical, as I pretended, lied, and created falsities for every question she asked during these prank sessions. Signed, Pitch Bel"

"I quit. Let's go get dinner." His face offered no indication that he was joking and I set down my pen and notepad.

"Where did you get this?" I asked wondering if it would be binding in court. I wasn't dating him, *ever,* but my mind went there anyway.

"The Bankers. My brethren get free advice from

the Fathers' bankers for life. It's real. Keep it, it's yours. Let's go out. Kfir's at church."

I shook my head, re-reading the letter. "I don't want to date you, Pitch. I don't like you."

"Right," he replied with a *pshaw.* **"You like me just fine. You only want me to be nice, like little Kfir."**

I met his eye and was sorry I had. I didn't want to be obvious, to be *read.* I wanted him to always be guessing, but so far, I sucked at hiding my thoughts.

"How about this, since I'm not a patient, let me help you with your Rakum model. With him in church all the time, I could pinch hit."

I didn't trust him. The image of him mimicking sex with his hands at the elevator Monday night, looking me dead in the eye and mocking me to my face. Mocking my pain and my horrendous past after stealing and reading my personal and confidential files. What kind of superwoman would I need to be to forget that?

"You don't trust me." Pitch put his hands to his hips and looked about the room in a thoughtful manner. When he had circuited the office, he landed back in my gaze with a half-grin. **"I'll prove myself. You think you know us, but your acquaintances haven't shown you my personality type. Am I right?"**

I couldn't disagree. Even those I met with El-A, none were as vile and openly nasty as Pitch had been before this night.

With a secretive wink, Pitch's fingers manipulated his phone screen and he spoke-to-texted, **"Plus one female."** When I continued to only stare on, he flashed the screen to my face. A website had been called up, its central shape, Keifer's new church. **"You in? In less than an hour, we can look in on this new hobby of Kfir's."** He waggled his eyebrows, amazingly manifesting opposite personality markers from the previous session.

No, not a session.

He has legal documents to prove it.

He's not my patient.

I scoffed inside. He didn't have to admit it, but he would always be a patient to me. He had anger issues, he wasn't born human, he would never be the same as my normal clients. But, so what? Do I ride with him to Tuscaloosa? I liked the idea of seeing Keifer, of getting a look at this church in person. Of finding out if I would lose him to God as Pitch said I would.

"Bring your voice recorder. A building filled with my brethren." He rolled his eyes with mock excitement. **"What things you will learn!"**

He had a point. My right hand reached for my coat off the chair and my left found and pocketed my recorder. He turned for the door, shrugging on a dark canvas pea coat. I did not see myself riding in his car. I also couldn't see myself chauffeuring him all the way to T-town.

Wait. He's a millionaire.

At the elevator, I cleared my throat and he looked back, brow raised. "Call us a car. A mortal company with a mortal driver."

I watched his face and he nodded, swiping pages on his cell as we loaded into the lift. My office is on the third floor so in a few seconds the door opened to the lobby. I waved to security and when my hand touched the exit, Pitch said the address into his phone. He hung up and showed me the call receipt: Iron City Luxury Limos.

"Good, thanks," I said, as if he was a normal associate.

"You're welcome," Pitch said, delivering the correct response.

I was impressed. Maybe he meant what he said. Maybe he "flipped the script" after all. I wanted it to be true, but he'd been so evil. I cleared my mind and we both strolled to the circle drive of the complex.

The night was cold, bordering on freezing and I shivered, wishing I'd worn my scarf. Bundled in a sufficient Northface jacket and I'd worn leather boots, the only thing truly cold was my face and I covered my nose.

"Empathy test number two," Pitch said a laugh in his voice as he pulled a black leather glove from his pocket.

As he passed it over, he used both hands to turn its palm inside-out—it was lined with snow-white rabbit fur. I grinned despite myself and moved aside a bright orange care instructions tag sewn inside and pressed the downy warmth to my nose tip. I wanted to thank him, to tell him *good job*, reveal that he had impressed me, but I didn't. His grinning face and hard, reptilian gaze from Monday night, reminded me to hold my cards close.

Rakum don't need polite responses and he hadn't waited around for a thank you. He flagged the limo as it rounded the turn and when it inched to a stop before us, Pitch opened the back door before the driver could make it around. I slipped into the backseat and trained my gaze to the chauffeur. I wanted to be sure he was mortal. I can't always tell, I mean, I don't think any mortal can see them as well as they see each other. If seen out of context, a man moves too smoothly and looks a little, well, too aquiline, I wonder if he's Rakum. The only context I had for our driver was Pitch's word and what I presume is a mortal-run company driver. When the stranger met my eye to nod a greeting, I didn't see anything to suspect him. The limo was a stretch and Pitch positioned across from me facing front where I was sitting with my back to the partition.

Once underway and pulling into traffic, I tapped the glass behind my head. "Does this open?" I asked the air and in a quiet swish, a third of the tempered glass between myself and the driver disappeared. I looked at the driver's profile and said, "Leave this open, please."

After his confused sideways agreement, I settled in my seat, facing the Rakum.

Pitch, not a human patient, not a friend. Should I accept his proposal and become associates? How would Keifer feel about that? I huffed—my lover is still too Rakum to experience the type of jealousy we do. *Keifer.* I wondered how it would play out at church. Would he be angry I came? Did it matter?

Pitch didn't speak and he didn't stare at me. He leaned comfortably back and gazed out his window. My phone chimed and I peeked at the screen. Since Patient 7 became a focus, I set my phone to send alerts when a story occurs with my chosen keywords.

Parents Seek Justice, Holy Ground Homicide

My skin prickled as the memory of Jenny's newspaper clipping came to mind. I opened the article and read the first sentence.

> *Parents of Jocelyn Peterson asking all citizens of Holy Ground, Alabama, to help find the person responsible for the murder of their daughter..."*

I scanned for the watchword I sought and it came toward the end of the report.

> *"Peterson, 28, was born a male and living as a female seven years leading up to her..."*

No mention of the tongue, but the rest? It had to be the same killer. I rolled in my lips. This guy's body count was rising, and the bodies found too close to home. Holy Ground Battlefield Park, where the body was located, was only thirty miles from my office.

To my delight, Pitch did not pry, and I put my phone away. Forty-five miles to Tuscaloosa. Okay. I stared out my window and tried not to think too hard.

The Hitch with Pitch

Not too surprisingly, the guards at the church gate let us through. Pitch didn't recognize the Rakum, but he said the right words in their language. In as much as I could see in the darkened landscape, I marveled at the meticulous care given to every shrub, tree, and curb. White criss-cross horse fencing lined both sides of the drive causing me to want to see it in the day—maybe they had horses. I'm not a rider, but what little girl doesn't dream of a black stallion to solve all her woes?

The church cube sat illuminated by LED lamps directed to its four corners and front door. Parking slots lined both sides, and besides a plain white work van, each spot housed a luxury vehicle of some sort. I had to snicker; the Rakum loved to spend money as much as the rest of us.

The driver let us out, intending I guess to pull around and wait for us to be finished. Pitch and I made meaningless remarks before we stopped at the entrance. With a tiny glance at my face, he pushed the door handle and waltzed in. I paused holding the door open and peering into the gigantic room. Kiefer was nowhere in sight.

"Ah! It's Pitch!" a man's voice barked and approached without meeting my eye. He got right into Pitch's space and swung a left hook. Maybe for a millisecond I thought a negative event had occurred, but I recovered having learned this was a proper greeting among many of them. If they didn't screw, they greeted each other with violence.

"You look well, muthafukka," Pitch said, pronouncing the curse with humor as he dodged the offender's blow and delivered a vicious upper cut to his chin. The strike made contact and his brother spiraled backward, laughing and bringing one hand to his face even as he tumbled ass-down to the tile. The man on the floor glanced at me and asked Pitch a question in their language. Pitch answered in English, translating, which was nice.

"This is Kfir's mate. Where's he hiding?" Pitch asked and didn't offer to help the Rakum to his feet. I watched the guy scramble to standing position, massaging his jaw as he continued the conversation.

"Unloading some shit with Walker." The Rakum hooked a thumb backward and looked to me. "Kfir's woman..." He turned to Pitch and finished in their language, his tone indicating he didn't like me, or maybe women in general.

As I had grown accustomed, they spoke several minutes in Rakum Hungarian as if I didn't exist. I allowed my mind to wander. I didn't feel comfortable walking away, so from where I stood, I put my hands behind my back and drank it in. I studied the other men, the bema at the front, and the floor and the ceiling. I was about to start the circuit all over again when a mountain of something amazing walked in from a back hall.

It was a man—a Rakum—but there was something different about him. I'll break it down. He swaggered in, *truly,* as if in his mind, everyone was watching, adoring, and worshipping him. Wait… I guess I worshipped him a little, studying his walk, his build, the way his hair hung to his chin and swayed with each step. Holy shit, his profile and then ¾-face had my stomach doing flip-flops. He stopped at a collection of his brothers, stood three and four inches over all of them. He nodded and chuckled and although I couldn't hear his voice, his laugh was deep. One of his brothers lifted a hand to his neck and squeezed. The Adonis's reaction was to lean down to press his face in. From my angle, it could have been a whisper, a kiss, or a bite but he held their faces like that a few seconds.

Oh, geez.

He looked up and locked eyes with me.

This man had yellow eyes—no shit. Even from twenty yards, they shimmered as if they were supposed to be hazel but ended up without enough melatonin. Whatever the cause, they were bright. I nodded, reflecting his movement, and he started toward me. With my eyes wide, I glanced at Pitch. He was still engaged with the man he hadn't introduced. Sexy eyes reached me and he put out a hand.

"My name is Darcy," he said and I loved his voice with my whole heart. "You're surely not with Pitch, so…" he said and when I gave him my hand, he lifted it and tenderly pecked the outside. "What's your story?"

I offered a polite smile and in my peripheral vision, Pitch noticed and closed his conversation. He turned to put his arm about my shoulders and face the taller man.

"Move along, Vandiver," Pitch said and rolled his hand. "She has enough _____" Pitch finished in their language.

Darcy Vandiver. Now I had his entire name and it seemed to rhyme in my head.

"I'll take you to Kfir," he said with a bow, putting out an elbow in a gesture you might see in a black and white film. I didn't accept. He was accustomed to yes, so I tossed him a no. His brow lifted and he smiled. "You prefer I move along?" he asked, his voice indicating he'd do it. He didn't need me and was only being polite. I remembered he was a Rakum and answered forthrightly.

"I'll wait with Pitch. Thanks."

The man's smile remained, and he held my eye two more seconds. Then he nodded in a graceful and tiny bow before turning away. I watched him go, every cell in my body wanting to know him better.

Kiefer entered and they met as he walked my way. I watched for their greeting—touch. *Ah.* And a kiss to the jaw. *Shit.* Another man I should wonder if my lover's sleeping with. Kiefer passed him and met my eye with a new grin.

"What is this?" he asked, his eyes jumping between mine and Pitch's. When he was close enough, he greeted me in the mortal fashion – pecked my mouth and slid his hand down my arm from bicep to wrist to hold my fingers. This was progress.

"Pitch offered to bring me. This is very interesting," I said with a glance to each corner. "This is where a Rakum meets God."

Kiefer chuckled once and his eyes flashed with humor (or maybe it was affection. I am not as sure with this new thing he's doing). "Let me introduce you around," he said and turned away, holding my hand.

Then, for fifteen minutes, my boyfriend walked me through the groups, speaking English, and his brethren followed his lead. Pitch did not join us, but disappeared to do his own thing. When Keifer and I had made the circuit, he stopped at the front near a podium and the one called David Walker approached.

"And here's David," Kiefer said, and I gave the man a nod. As I noted when I saw him in the photo, I'd never seen any Rakum like him. I suppose the oddest thing, Rakum-wise, was his expression. He just looked *sweet*. If I'd seen him first out in the world, I never would have pegged him as a Rakum.

After he made a comment regarding the schedule, he grinned and caught my eye. "Say it... Your face..."

Keifer turned to see my expression and his brow lifted. "Yes, what is it?"

Amazed that I was so easy to read I waved one hand. "I was thinking you look nothing like a Rakum. I don't mean it as an insult, but I've met probably a hundred, and you, well..." I shrugged one shoulder. As I expected, the man was not offended.

"Hah," he said with a knowing grin to Keifer. "I never fit in with my brothers. Now that I follow the Maker, I realize He made me this way for a purpose."

Keifer nodded in agreement but I didn't want to remark. Nothing about church or God interested me in the least.

"We just finished the service," David said allowing the previous topic to drop. "Do you want to sit-in on some small groups? Kfir tells us you're a psychologist working to help my brothers assimilate. I would enjoy being part of that. Perhaps we can share contact information. If a brother comes to either of us for something we can help with, we'll refer them over."

"Like if he's sociopathic, you'll send him to me, and if he wants to know about God, send him to you?" I asked in what I thought sounded like a polite tone.

71

Walker nodded with a friendly smile. "Precisely." He tipped a chin to Pitch. "Be cautious spending your time with him. Kfir informed me of his promise, but he's not trustworthy." David turned his face to Keifer. "Does she know his specialty before?"

Keifer took my hand in his. "Pitch is a seduction and torture expert. Men and women the Master wanted chastised or ended, Pitch would be sent to draw them close enough to grab without attracting authorities." With a gentle grin, Kiefer lifted his hand to move my hair behind my ear. "But he will not break his vow to me; he won't touch you without consent."

"If you consent," David Walker added stepping in and lowering his voice, "he won't be gentle. If you were his mate instead of Kfir's, he'd prefer to rape you than make love. Do you understand what I am saying? For however long your association persists, he will seek to seduce and conquer you—his way."

I squirmed under their scrutiny, Keifer and David Walker both waiting for me to answer in the affirmative, that I wouldn't trust him, I promise, etc. And I believed them, *but they're working me so hard...* I nodded and a movement to the back door caught my attention. I looked over and Darcy Vandiver had reentered. In the three seconds in my gaze, his bright eyes flicked up and he sent me a nod. Shit, my blood rushed downward and I jerked my head to the side.

"I appreciate that, but I told Keifer, I don't want Pitch to touch me, *ever,*" I said and shook my head. "Anyway, I have a boyfriend." I looked up to Keifer who then brought me into his chest and leaned down to kiss my forehead.

"You left this in the shitter," a man's smooth voice sounded behind us and I turned my face.

72

It was Ivan and he handed Keifer a Bible. My eye twitched; he'd come from outside. Specifically, the front parking lot. Was Ivan putting my love up at his place all this time? Were they "playing their favorite games"?…

Goddammit, Ruth.

"When will you be home?" I asked with the softest eyes I could muster.

"I don't know yet," he answered with a glance to Walker. "Not this week."

I huffed and did not hide it well. I would need to be candid; Rakum did not understand mind games. I ordered my thoughts. Think about it; females don't speak forthrightly. It doesn't come naturally or easily; everything we say and do has an ulterior motive. Not that its bad or good, its simply the way we're built. We must protect the treasure we keep between our legs, and protecting that treasure involves careful control of the dicks around us.

I took a deep breath and said in an even, non-emotional tone, "I want you to come home now. I want you to study this God thing a different way so we can be together every night like before. I don't like this separation."

Keifer gave me a thoughtful nod, his eyes dancing between Walker, Ivan, and me.

"Do the mortal thing and come home," I added as if the topic was closed.

"The mortal thing?" Keifer asked and his eyes narrowed. "Do you believe in the Maker?"

Ugh. The question came right out of his beautiful mouth. Did I believe in God? Yes. Did I believe in Keifer's version of God? No. I answered the best way I could.

"I don't know Him like you do." Then I added when he did not comment right away, "I don't think it's right to set me aside for this."

Keifer took a deep breath and exhaled slow, his eyes in mine and then turning to David Walker. He said a phrase to the preacher in their language and shook his head.

"Kfir spent his life as a soldier, answering to Pitch and the other captains," David said to me and I only met his gaze when he resumed after that last word. "He was highly regarded among them because he was decisive and confident in his every military choice."

I rolled my eye, guessing where he was headed, but I held my tongue.

"Now that he's mortal, he still listens to his instincts. When his conscience tells him to perform a thing, now that he knows the Maker, he pauses and runs the deed past the Maker's Word and the teachings he's had here among us. He asked if you believed because this is how we judge who to listen to for advice."

I huffed. He was about to insult me, but again I clenched my jaw without a word.

"As a non-believer, your opinions carry less weight than those of the newest follower of the Maker. When we believe, God's Spirit comes to live inside us and nudges us down the path we should take. You either don't have that Spirit or you have squashed Him for whatever reason…"

"*F-u-u-u-c-c-k-k-k,*" Pitch said with mock exasperation walking into the circle. "Come on, doll-face. I'll run you back. I think we've heard enough of this fairytale shit."

"I'll only take as long as necessary," Keifer said to me and I met his eye. "I want to be with you too. I miss you." He made a tiny grin and cupped my cheek. "That sounds like a great human sentiment and I mean it."

"I know you do," I said, defeated. "Just hurry."

The four of us made a turn and started for the front

74

doors while Ivan went the opposite direction. A few of the others called goodbyes to Pitch and in another minute we were in the lot watching the hired car drive into position to load up.

Keifer took me into his arms and hugged me, his chin resting atop my head. I held on, my arms around his ribcage, my fingers spread to take miniscule examinations of his muscular back. I hadn't had sex in four days, and that was a long time for us. Since I met Keifer, he was never short on libido.

His embrace turned platonic and when I lifted my face for a kiss, the peck he offered lasted less than a millisecond. When the driver opened the back door and I piled in with Pitch directly behind, I sat in the bench seat to watch Kiefer through the window. He had already turned, the goodbyes done, and was entering the building. Ivan met him in the entrance and walked him the rest of the way under his wing, speaking close.

God, I hate that church, I said inside and maybe under my breath, because Pitch huffed what sounded like agreement.

The Ride Home

I closed the partition before the driver had settled behind the wheel, and I didn't look at Pitch. He sat where he had on the ride up and I dropped my weight also on the forward-facing bench, on the opposite side of the car, and stared out my window as we got underway. I sensed Pitch's eyes on the back of my head. He wanted to comment. Why didn't he? If he wanted to hurt me, now would be an excellent time. My defenses had been completely erased and I didn't see rebuilding the ramparts for a very long time. Yet, he remained silent.

Five minutes into the ride, I was sick of the quiet. Still staring into the night on my side of the limo, I asked, "Do they have sex in there? In a mortal church building, sex is prohibited."

I swiveled to see if he had an answer. Keifer's brothers touched each other's necks one-handed, like mortals might shake hands or hug. But the way Darcy Vandiver melted low to press his lips to more than one jaw—it appeared a sexual thing. Pitch hadn't replied and, in the darkness, I only saw the reflection off his eyes.

"Who is Darcy Vandiver to Keifer?" I asked thinking a new question wouldn't hurt.

"Darcy Vandiver," Pitch responded, dragging out the syllables with a mysterious grin. "Before the end of the world, his job was fucking, sucking, and fighting, and he did it all with utter perfection."

I leaned back, facing front. "His literal job?" I knew Rakum did not mince words, but the guy's occupation was screwing?

"Yeah, all of us had a job. Vandiver is what we called *ish-mikhan*." He looked over, as if I should say the foreign word. I did and he continued. "It means 'fix-it man.' He was born with innate hypersexual abilities." Pitch smiled when I huffed, his teeth reflecting in the passing lights. "In case you run across one in your treatment, their behavior was always more human; they're more capable of empathy." He gave another grin. "This gave them the ability to guess with accuracy what a brother needed in any department. Darcy can fix anything any of us would ever need in the realm of pleasure or violence."

"That's just... I keep learning the craziest stuff."

Pitch chuckled deep and private. After a moment he said to the side, "The Elders had a pet name for the ish-mikhan. When he hears it, his flashbacks get him hard as a rock. Call Darcy *polsc-v'* and he'll do anything you ask."

I rolled my gaze out the window. I didn't want anything from the giant sexpert, I wanted Keifer. "He was great at sex. Got it."

"He's also a soldier and we spent some years together on assignment. We were compatible."

"You're all compatible," I whispered to the air. It was childish, but I was mad. Pitch thought I was serious.

"No, we're not. The guy I clocked? I'd never put my

lips on that shit."

"Do you think they have sex in the Rakum church?" I asked with no energy in my voice. I had seen the Rakum screwing each other in my days with El-A, but I had put that behind me. I assumed Keifer had, too.

"Probably not," he replied, and I don't think he's capable of lying to make me feel better. "But I recognized a lot of those guys from my rowdy days." He got no reaction from me and continued with a harmless smirk. "Vandiver's the king of the fuck, but if he wasn't around, there are several there who can blow a man's mind. But to answer your question, none of my brethren demonstrated any pre-fuck behavior while we were there."

He had spoken the last part with a laugh and then flipped a tiny light in his side of the car. It illuminated with a pink hue and I saw his mirth. It was friendly, *human,* and I relaxed a fraction in my posture and my tone.

"Thank you, you know..." I shrugged. "For all of it."

Pitch made a *hmph* noise and nothing more. The car had grown toasty and I tugged my inside sleeve to remove my coat. Pitch's fingers found the cuff and he helped, pulling in tiny jerks until my coat was off. I thanked him without turning and tossed it onto the seat across. In my peripheral vision, Pitch's outstretched fingers came into view. Puzzled, I looked at his face; he wore a tiny grin and wiggled four digits in my direction. With a huff and a small smile, I helped him off with his jacket in a similar manner. When he flipped his atop mine, he relaxed back and kicked out his legs with a contented sigh.

"Comfy?" I said with muted humor. He had shown immense self-control tonight, more than ever proving the Pitch I met in those first three sessions was not the true man. Maybe he was more like Keifer than I had realized.

78

Maybe Keifer simply knew better how to express his mortal side. Why not? Rakum-turned-mortal psychology was in its infancy and I was at the forefront of the research. I considered that as he sighed and turned his gaze to mine.

"Yeah," he responded to my question after a deep yawn. "Try it," he said and watched to see if I would.

With little forethought, I did. I slumped down, my butt sliding forward to the edge of the leather seat, my legs out long, and chin to my breastbone. I chuckled at the sight of my middle folded over, causing false fat rolls in my sweater. Pitch followed my line of sight and in the corner of my eye, he grinned.

"Fat little beauty queen," he said low, his smile belying the joke. "Look at that gut."

At his second line, he slumped another inch and forced his belly out to cause a bulge. He was tight across his middle like Keifer and his shirt thin and forgiving, but I laughed and pointed.

When he chuckled I raised my eyes and caught his gaze. Those eyes, hazel-green, bright and shimmering, reflecting the passing car headlights and intermittent streetlamps. He blinked slow and licked his lips.

"He was right, you know," Pitch said in a soft voice, seductive and I think he meant it that way. "You are different. I wonder why…"

"What do you mean?" I asked at the same volume.

"Every female wants to be the one that turns the prince's eye, but you actually did. Kfir, Ivan, David, every brother in that building… Me, when I first saw you."

"You're exaggerating," I said and looked at my hands folded on my middle. The men in Keifer's fellowship had been polite, but were they all thinking this? That their brother had found a princess?

"Don't play modest with me. You know we don't like that." He *tsked*, but his smile remained. And he was right — I knew better.

"Well, if I stand out to the..." I stopped before I said Rakum, unsure if the driver could hear us. "If I stand out, maybe it has to do with ya'll. With what you look for or are expecting in females."

"Let's add that to our investigation," he said and scooted into a more upright position.

My mind fuzzed and I guess it showed on my face because Pitch explained his statement with a patient grin.

"With Kfir preoccupied with the Maker, I'm going to be your connection to the brethren. I will help you build the model for your practice." He watched my face and I held it still. "Did you think I was joking when we discussed this?"

"No, but I don't think Keifer's out. He's just..." I tried to think of the right words. Once he's done with this part, he'd be spending a few nights a week in Tuscaloosa, but other than that, he should be home with me, right? He hadn't dumped me; he just asked for some time. I looked within myself and asked, right?

"Doll-face, really," Pitch said then, his voice eerily similar to Keifer's. I found it interesting how accurately he mimicked him; was he doing that on purpose? Pitch lifted his cell and pressed a phone number. I heard the answer in the small space.

"Kazak. Ya'll get off okay?" Keifer's voice. I sat upright as Pitch had and put out my hand for the phone. Pitch held it beyond reach with a teasing grin.

"Nice choice of words, brother," Pitch replied and I made another useless grab for the phone. "Is this your woman? It seems you released her tonight, but she's not

80

sure."

"What? Olsc'v pultz-kitit—" Kiefer spoke their language and Pitch interrupted.

"In English, Kfir. Go ahead. She's listening."

"Put her on the phone," Keifer said. *"I'm not talking to her through you."* With that devilish grin in place, Pitch handed over the cell.

"Hey," I said and couldn't think of a better greeting.

"What prompted this? Are you having a new opinion on my doings—an opinion that differs from the one you gave me before you left?"

I watched Pitch's face as Keifer spoke. It was so easy for them to lie and even easier for them to speak plainly. For me, both came with a measure of forethought. I took too long and Keifer continued.

"When a brother uses that term, *released,* it means he wants a stab at you. Is that what you want? Are you alone with Pitch wanting to…"

"No, stop," I said at volume and then hushed to a whisper. "No, I want you."

"I'm sure that's true, but let's stop with the games. I'm happy to share you with Pitch—he's my closest companion of the Old Way, and no matter what David thinks, he's no danger to you. Lean on him when I'm gone. I'll be back as soon as it's right and tell me then what you want to do. From a mortal perspective, I understand this is screwed up, but listen…" Keifer's voice softened to finish with, "I treasure you. I also treasure this new adventure in Tuscaloosa."

"Okay," I said sounding all of twelve years old.

Pitch removed the phone from my hand and spoke a few sentences in their language before Keifer answered his brother in English saying, *"Only by consent."*

81

Pitch dropped his phone into a slot in the door handle and shot me a killer smile, his handsome face so dramatic in the varying light.

"What was that last part? What's the context for the consent thing?" I asked my voice small.

Pitch licked his lips slow and with purpose. "I asked him some tips on what you like in bed."

My jaw dropped. "No, you didn't," I said, but of course he did. What else would a Rakum ask his brother when given permission to have sex with his mate?

"How about it? It starts with a kiss." Pitch slipped closer by a few inches, although we still sat nearly two feet apart in the huge car.

"No," I said but didn't slide away and I held his gaze.

The audacity. Keifer thinks he can *share* me like El-A did a million years ago. As if I was a thing, a tool, a bottle of milk. He was learning to be human, but both men had a long way to go.

Pitch inched in and my eyes flit to his black hair, wavy and begging to be grasped in feminine fists. His proper beard thicker than Keifer's, long enough that I could bury my fingers in the coarse facial hair to pull our faces together. His lips were full, no more alluring than Keifer's but Pitch parted them then and his tongue peeked out to wet them once.

His tongue.

Abusive and hurtful two nights ago.

"You are a beautiful woman," Pitch said then, his voice as silky as any I'd ever heard. His eyes jumped about as mine did, examining my lips, my hair, my throat, my chest. I had the feeling he might be imagining similar things as I was. Why not ask him? He'd answer straight.

"What are you thinking about?" My voice came out a

82

rasp and I couldn't change the fact that my heartrate was up and worse, my lower body had switched on to prepare for action.

"I was thinking that everything you like about my brother you will like a hundred times better in me."

I blinked. "You believe that, eh?"

"Kfir said don't tickle, but run my palm down your back, cup your buttocks with both hands and squeeze, hard."

I swallowed, not realizing he'd go right there and talk details. I had to be as tough as he was, so I added, "What else?"

"He said if I run one hand all the way around, from behind, and into your body, one, two, and then three fingers, it drives you insane."

Pitch's voice could not be more seductive and as he finished those words, his palm conformed to my thigh. I swallowed, my mind so there, imagining this beautiful man nude, propped over me and fulfilling me with careful fingers, in every way I enjoyed.

"How 'bout it, doll-face," he said low.

"I don't like that name," I said sounding stupid. "Try another one." I leaned close then and didn't kiss him, just leaned close enough to do so—if he called me an endearment I liked. I am after all, in charge of my body.

Pitch grinned. "Let me make love to you."

"Back at my office, you said you'd fuck me and leave," I said still in a near whisper, watching his eyes, our mouths so close we breathed the same air.

"I say a lot of things," he breathed and ended with, "Ruthy."

I snapped out of my trance—the fucker was still only wooing me for his purposes. I had been used plenty and this turd wasn't going on that list; not if I could help it. With an angry sigh I pushed violently away and slammed my knuckles against the Pyrex partition. It opened and I shouted for the driver to pull over. As he did so, I slid on my coat and rearranged my clothing. Pitch watched all of this without expression and I threw open the door when I felt the car almost at a halt.

Where were we? I took one glance—it was bitter cold and wisps of a snow-tease fluttered on the dry wind. We were downtown and I noted the Popeye's Chicken two blocks ahead. My office was one block beyond that. I started walking. The driver called after me and I waved behind my head. I had taken a good ten strides when another man's deep voice called over the night sounds, "Dr. Angleton?"

I turned to see Darcy Vandiver calling to me across the width of his jacked-up red dually Ford.

"Kfir sent me to make sure you get home okay," he continued, maneuvering his vehicle to the curb, ahead of the still quiet hired car. "Can I give you a lift?"

I looked back at the limo; Pitch hadn't stepped out. The driver stood waiting and watching me and Darcy. With only a moment's hesitation, I waved for the driver to leave and I climbed into Darcy's truck.

Kiefer sent him. This was good.

"You are a beautiful woman," Darcy said once he put the truck into gear, "with a natural, earthy countenance. The meat on your bones, soft-looking but intelligent and demure."

The drive would be short; I could see the outline of my office building. In another second, I'd see my car in my assigned spot.

"You shouldn't be surprised my brothers come on to

you." His eyes flicked in my direction and back to the road. I didn't look over, the shape of my Nissan growing larger by the moment. "I knew El-A very well. Have you wondered where he is?"

"No," I said without intention. I didn't want to talk about El-A, my questionable attractiveness to the Rakum, nor anything else the handsome devil might bring up. I wanted him to get me safely to my car, that's all.

"He was shot and killed by a drug dealer last summer," the man offered and slowed to park behind my car. "Be careful. It's icy."

I turned to see his face, his beautiful mouth in a sideways grin. "What? I know how to be polite," he said with a soft chuckle.

I grew curious about him then; what did he want from me? Anything? Nothing? What had Kiefer told him to do? I crossed my arms and did not exit the truck.

"Do ya'll have sex in the Rakum church?" I asked point blank, watching his face in the dash lights. He shook his head, his feathery chin-length hair moving in half-time. "Is Kiefer done with me? What did he tell you about me?"

Darcy leaned back and exhaled. It occurred to me that he might have had plans and I was slowing him down. A man with his looks probably didn't spend much time alone.

"Am I holding you up?"

He grinned my way and faced front again. "Kfir asked me to make sure you got safely to your car. Pitch gives off signals we recognize. None of us thought you capable of fending him off." He grinned sideways. "I'm impressed."

This time, I exhaled and with a half-shrug made a small *humph*. "I've dealt with much worse, trust me."

Darcy nodded as if he had knowledge. "We can see that, too. My brothers and I," he clarified. "We see your

85

psychological injuries based upon centuries of study. But I think Kfir must have told you all this." I nodded and watched his profile. "And I'm not magical any longer," he said with a peek my way, "so I can't promise anything regarding Kfir's feelings. But as of tonight, he is devoted to making your mate-up a success. My limited experience as a mortal says you need to be patient."

"I will. I am," I mumbled and put my fingers to the door handle. My eye caught sight of the hired car pulling up tight to Darcy's truck. I turned to see his eyes. "Are you going to talk to Pitch? Tell him to give me a week and then we'll start back up. I can help him. I know it."

"I'll tell him," the man replied and I longed to hear him say something else. His voice touched me so deep inside that I knew I'd use it to get off as I crawled into my bed alone.

"Are you sleeping with Pitch tonight?" I asked and knew he would be happy to tell me. All of the Rakum enjoyed talking about themselves and sex.

Darcy chuckled with a small nod. "He invited me over."

My mind toyed with that a split-second, undressing the giant beside me and watching him approach the strong and strapping Pitch with a smolder in his bright yellow eyes. It was enough, I'd use every bit of that tonight to help me forget how much I miss Kiefer in my bed.

I made a small goodbye and got out. I did NOT look back to the hired car but slid into my own vehicle and locked the doors. I revved the engine and Darcy Vandiver caught my eye in the rearview, him still in his truck, waiting to see if I'd leave. I did and drove away, leaving him and the devil to fuck or fight or whatever occurred to them. One thing was certain, I couldn't get home fast enough.

Two hours later, I lay in the dark looking at a sliver of light on the ceiling. I'd tickled myself twice already and still couldn't sleep. Counting invisible sheep, I almost dozed off when my phone buzzed. Once I'd opened the message center, I had an audio file from Pitch. What do you expect? I opened it.

"Polsc! Fuck! Let me go!"

My breath caught. It was Pitch and his voice was laughing. Who was he talking to? He chortled again and my instincts told me this had something to do with sex.

"Darss…"

"Be still," a deep voice followed atop Pitch's last word. *"You called me over here,"* the same voice continued. *"Now behave."*

Oh, God. That voice. My finger hovered over the red button. I should turn it off. Pitch was manipulating me. *Again.* The stop button, so easy to press.

But I didn't.

Scuffling and shuffling filled the recording. A chuckle, a huff, the clink of metal, as if a belt was tossed aside.

"Go to the bed, fuck!" Pitch's voice, still laughing with fake exasperation. Where were they? Then Pitch magically answered. *"No fucking in the foyer, Darss,"* he said, his breath hitching hard on the man's name as if he'd been struck.

"If you weren't such a Nancy, you'd be free to choose," Darcy replied, his voice urgent now. *"Be still, and shhh."*

My finger sat millimeters from STOP, but I listened. They were doing it. I looked at the phone, breathless. I imagined the scene, that perfect mountain of man astride Pitch, smaller in stature, but just as perfect in shape and overall sexiness. Darcy was on top, obvious by their banter, and Pitch was loving it, despite his complaints of earlier. I listened and listened until a loud grunt issued in a very deep vibrato.

My phone whirred and a banner slipped into view and rolled away. *Pitch: Video Link.* I took a deep breath but didn't notice until the exhale.

Shit. I'm a mental health professional. None of this means anything.

I pressed the link.

What looked like a security camera, its eye-view from a ceiling facing the front door. The entryway was longish, leaving room for a slender table on the right and a coat tree on the left at the doorway.

A movement at the glass in the door and it opened. Pitch walked in and made a tiny glance to the camera. Did he wink? It was too fast and I could rewind it later. I watched, morbidly interested in what he was sending. He took four steps in and stopped at the table, shuffling through what looked like mail. Then a second figure walked in, shoving the door closed behind him. Darcy Vandiver. My throat went dry. Was this? I didn't get to finish the inner query.

Darcy surged into Pitch and when they slapped together, Pitch swiveled to run away, which would have been toward the camera.

"Polsc! Shit!" he barked, grinning and absorbing a powerful hug-throw by his pal that had him against the wall. Darcy pinned him flat with his bodyweight, standing three inches taller, his arms up and palms pressed to the drywall. He spoke in Pitch's ear.

"Be still..." Darcy brought one hand off the wall to reach around to Pitch's front, his movements as if removing a belt. "You called me over here..."

Pitch's jeans loosened from the waist, gaping and Darcy focused now on his own fly, still pressing Pitch to the wall.

"Go to the bed, shit," Pitch said, flipping his face to my vantage, his eyes flicking to mine.

He's making this for me!

Darcy's far hand had moved to Pitch's back and moved low, beyond my vantage point. But his machinations brought expressions to Pitch's face. He cursed, licked his lips, complained incoherently and fell silent as the giant Adonis now kissed his ear and neck from behind, the hand I couldn't see massaging and bringing moans of need. At least he'd stopped looking at the camera. I needed to stop watching. Why did I watch?

Just set it down.

I turned the screen away and lifted my gaze to the room. In my hand, the deep voice of the fix-it man said, *"There you are, my beautiful, sexy man, easy..."*

I rotated the phone and whimpered. Darcy had Pitch on the shiny floor, atop him, covering and engulfing him as if he were three times bigger. They were both mostly clothed, but enough had been shed that they'd made a connection. A rhythmic and sensuous cadence had been struck, Darcy hovering near Pitch's ear, cooing sweet words to him. Pitch seemed to have forgotten the movie, his face to the floor, bracing on his forearms. From the ceiling, I saw only their backs, but I turned up the sound with my thumb, eyes locked to the dance.

"Do you want me to come, baby?" Darcy whispered. *"Say it, whatever you want, so sexy, so beautiful, just say what you want."*

"Yes, fuck!" Pitch said his volume elevated, but a mixture of emotions transmitted. *"Yes!"* And he grunted.

Darcy climaxed. The movement, even though

shrouded by unfastened trousers and hiked dress shirts, mesmerized me and I trained my eyes to their hips, Darcy's slowly coming to a stop and Pitch lowering himself to the floor as if in an exhale.

"You can go to the bed now, baby," Darcy said low, not disengaging, but draped over him, still erasing Pitch mostly from view. *"Say what you want."*

"Go to the bed," Pitch said and grimaced when his friend braced to roll off.

The resolution was amazing. Darcy Vandiver was circumcised—a rarity as I'd learned with El-A that the grunts weren't cut; only the Elders and Fathers held such a distinction. Add to this, his proportions were perfect, as if built for anyone.

He stood to his full height, trousers open and bunched in one fist, and he watched Pitch rise. Pitch's loosed jeans and shorts blocked my view of anything comparative and he walked toward my vantage and out of view without raising his eyes. I watched Darcy, mostly watching his erection, still semi-hard, bouncing with each step. He shrugged off his shirt without unbuttoning it revealing his ripped musculature. He was almost to the corner camera and he looked up.

Fuck.

He looked me right in the eye. His mouth tucked in on one side and he winked.

F-U-C-K.

Was that for me? Were they in it together? He passed out of view and the video ended. It rewound automatically and Pitch walked into his foyer.

"No!" I said to the empty room and shut off my phone. Pitch won again. And now I wondered…

Maybe Darcy wasn't the nice guy I had hoped he was.

10

The Chauffeur

It was Darcy Vandiver that stopped by before anyone else. Seven days came and went, me blowing off every client and barely making it to the shower each day. I wanted to disappear. Erase myself. But I didn't want to be dead; I only wanted the pain of my own inner worry to end. Keifer hadn't called or texted and I held his parting words spoken at the church close to my heart. *"I want you. But I want this too. If you will wait, I can have both."*

It was a lot of "I" statements, selfish, self-centered, but he was a new human. Wasn't that one of the things I loved about him? When the doorbell buzzed tonight, I hadn't expected Darcy. I peered through the peephole and looking to the side, Darcy stood, turning his face milliseconds before I stepped away from the eyepiece. Then he waved his fingers as if he saw me.

"What are you doing here?" I asked once the door was open. "Keifer okay?"

"He's fine. He asked me to give you an update since I was coming through on business."

I stood quiet a moment and didn't invite him in. Why should I? He could inform me from the doorway, right? He smiled then and blood rushed downward. Shit. I was lonely. I took a step backward and asked him to come in. He did after a tiny bow and followed me to the den. I had showered only an hour earlier and my hair was damp. I only realized this because he looked so together—hair perfect and soft, reflecting the light, his darkish complexion complimenting his emerald green turtleneck sweater and damn, those tailored gray slacks and shiny dress boots.

I miss Kiefer so bad!

"He wants you to come to Tuscaloosa. He has a hotel room reserved."

Darcy hadn't sat and neither had I. I was ready to go now—pack my bags, dump the rest of my week—shit, I could quit altogether. My client sheet is shorter than ever, can't I push my other regulars onto Jenny? How much money do I have saved up? If I stay with Keifer, he's a millionaire... doesn't that mean neither of us need to work?

"Are you going back there tonight?" I asked and then added like a bitch, "or are you having another slumber party with Pitch?"

He smiled and I melted a little more inside.

I need Kiefer!

"I'm headed back," he said and his hands tucked into his pockets. "Let me take you to dinner. You're not eating enough."

I shook my head. I was down a few pounds since last week, but it was mostly water weight. When you stay in bed sixteen hours a day on end, you get dehydrated. I crossed to the kitchen bar and scooped up my cell. I hit Kiefer's number and he picked up, sounding as if we had only spoken moments ago and not eight days.

"Hey, baby. Darss came by? Can you come up here? It'd be easier than me coming there. I'm really getting the hang of this thing."

I wanted to snark, *what thing? The Jesus-thing?* But I didn't. He wanted me close. Dozens of beautiful and perfect brethren on his every side and lord knows any female that caught sight of him would throw herself at his feet. Yet, he wanted me. And he told Pitch I'm the only one in the world that gives him peace of mind. That's got to count for something—if not everything.

"Sure, I want to see you," I said, sounding chipper. "I miss you. *A lot.*"

My voice carried a sexual overtone that Kiefer caught. He purred a little sound he made only when we made love.

"Let me speak to Darss."

I handed over the phone and the tall Rakum put it on speaker. "Kazak."

"Did you see Pitch?" he asked and I heard him plainly from where I stood.

"Not here. No one's seen him," Darcy replied.

"How was he when you saw him last?" Keifer asked, and it occurred to me they were speaking English for my benefit.

"Insatiable and irascible," Darcy replied with an apologetic wink my way, as if I'd be offended.

Huh. I didn't care. Kiefer asked a few more mundane questions and was gone. Darcy handed me the phone, his gaze asking, what now?

"Let me pack a little bag," I said and turned for the stairs. Darcy followed and halfway up, I stopped moving and looked back. "You can wait downstairs." He grinned and I did, too, my walls going down. Nothing about him frightened me. Why was that? I waved him up. "On second thought, come on and keep me company."

Darcy resumed climbing the stairs and once in the bedroom, he leaned on the doorframe as I packed a few items.

"Keifer asked me to check on Patient 7. Is that what you're calling the killer?"

I nodded. "He's been coming to one of my colleagues for his anger issues and admitted to her that he was the one killing these poor women." I looked up to see his face. "Do you know who it is?"

Darcy didn't say no, but the sides of his mouth turned down as he shrugged. I thought of Keifer's question to him on the phone.

"What about Pitch? He okay? You said he was missing?"

"He's not home and hasn't returned my calls," Darcy answered with a new shrug. "My brothers return my calls, trust me. I'm concerned. Kfir's concerned. Our brethren are so few in number..."

He stopped, but I heard the rest inside—*we need to watch out for each other.* Kiefer said that to me more than once.

"Keifer said they lived together in Columbus. Could he be there?" Even as I asked my question, for the first time, my mind went to the serial killer's victim in Corinth, Mississippi. *Wait. Where was Pitch each time these women were murdered? And didn't he leave our session early once or twice the night before a body was found?*

Maybe my face froze because Darcy's eyes widened.

"Ruth, take my word for it, Pitch is not killing these people. I am a hundred percent confident in this." Darcy said his statements watching my face. "Let's get going."

94

I didn't argue, but as I followed him down the stairs, dropped food for the cat and locked the front door, my mind picked apart the calendar and all the days my patient had unaccounted.

Darcy drove one of those good-ol-boy dually pickup trucks, this one ruby red with a nifty retractable step. It was posh, with all the bells and whistles and rode like a land yacht. Darcy did not talk unless I asked him a question, and the only thing on my mind was how Pitch called him a Sexpert. What the hell? I thought I'd ask him about it. I was horny and his deep voice, *damn!*

"Pitch explained this fix-it man thing. I'm fascinated to think this was your actual purpose—to screw?"

Darcy didn't turn, but he licked his lips and hummed, giving me the impression that he was his very favorite subject. I waited and he chuckled with a small shake of the head.

"For science?" he asked.

I didn't get it at first but then remembered my Rakum model. I said, sure.

"I was born with a special aptitude to bring my masters pleasure. It morphed into sex in due time, but it was always about knowing what my master wanted at any given time."

I said, *Hmm,* and pondered what he shared. Kiefer didn't spend much time with his Elder, they were given assignments and he would see him only on occasion. Keifer is one of those who told me they were assholes, so now I grinned, and Darcy noticed.

"Say it," he said with a peek my way.

"No, there's nothing," I stumbled over my reply for no good reason. "I'm learning, that's all. Keifer didn't like his Elder and neither did El-A." I shrugged. "I think it's interesting that you liked them."

"Liked?" he said with a peek my way. "Oh, I adored them, all of them." He *tsked* with a wry shake of the head, his hand absently pressing his crotch and returning to the armrest. "I was *born* for them."

His intonation piqued my curiosity. He wasn't kidding; he loved them and with a depth of emotion that I needed to add to my model. I asked him if he would allow me to interview him for that purpose and he shook his head.

"At Last Assembly, there were only four fix-it men left and I can attest that none of us are depressed."

Then he laughed and I asked him why. Darcy wiped his face with one huge hand.

"My brother Hester," he said inside a chuckle. "He's not depressed, he loves himself too much for that. But maybe you could help him stop being an ass."

Darcy laughed low and private and I did not dig, feeling he wouldn't say more anyway. I opened the voice recorder app and spoke this information in a new file. I asked him, "What's the Rakum word again? For fix-it man?"

"*Ish-mikhan.* We are loved by everyone. None of us would ever be sad enough to need your help."

I showed him the screen with a little wiggle. "Can I interview you about it?"

"I don't do interviews, Doc." He swiveled his face to mine long enough to wink. "I'll put it in my memoir.[4] You can read that if you're curious."

I nodded, wondering at the details. "It's hard to believe you're never depressed." I sucked my teeth in thought and asked, "How about angry? Keifer said all of you were filled with rage over what happened on 11/13."

He said nothing, looking at the road ahead.

"Were you angry?" I pressed.

Darcy made no indication he heard. With a sigh, I spoke that into my recorder, that Darcy Vandiver refused to answer my question, 'were you angry.' Overhearing me, his mouth tucked into a wry smile, but he remained quiet.

After two minutes of silence, Darcy turned on the radio. I pondered his perspective. If I ever get a minute alone with Kiefer, I'm going to ask him more about the ish-mikhan.

Wait.

The image of Darcy kissing Keifer's jaw popped up and I reached across the truck to tap his forearm. "Did you and Keifer used to sleep together?"

He looked at me a moment and then back out the windshield. "I've slept with most of the Rakum you've met. In three hundred years, I've had plenty of partners."

I only nodded and looked out my side of the car. Twenty minutes to Tuscaloosa. I found myself picturing Keifer's face, his chest, his so-fuzzy-middle that I loved to stroke before diving in properly.

Darcy and Keifer.

I let the image roll in, and I bided my time.

11

The Confederate

"He's not gonna stop. They need to find that asshole and cut off his dick," a heavyset woman in the corner said, not guarding her words or lowering her volume. I had stopped in for a trim, killing time until Keifer returned from whatever services he attended.

When Darcy brought me to the hotel room, Keifer had been waiting and he took me to bed right then. For the next hour, I wallowed in the most luxurious and delightful lovemaking of my life. But as soon as breakfast disappeared, so did my lover. Now I was stuck in T-town with no car and nothing to do. The hair salon sat in a shopping center adjacent to the room so I went for a walk. Did I mention it was February and icy? Yes, I froze my ass off and when Keifer gets home from church, I'll tell him *allllll* about it.

"I say cut it off and stick a broken bottle up his arse! And takin' their tongues? *Shite!*"

This woman's voice carried a Scottish accent and I peeked over. She had blue hair—yes, dyed robin-egg blue—and she must have been in her sixties. Her eyes darted to mine.

"Sweetness, you be careful out there. Some loon has killed a woman right here in town! Stay safe!"

I said I would and looked to the magazine in my hands. The women continued to discuss the killer and my depression grew. Was it Pitch? I had mapped the days I could pinpoint his location which was circumstantial evidence at best. I mean, if he's not with me, there are a zillion places he could go. It didn't mean...

"He hates gays," the first lady said as if the topic needed nothing added.

"He hates *transgendered* women, honey," her hairdresser corrected, lowering her voice only a tad on the watchword. "They have a witness."

"Yeah, some guy in the college bookstore. Why didn't he help? I don't see how his story holds water."

"I believe 'im," the Scot replied.

I hadn't heard anything about a witness and I waited to see if they'd expound. The hairdresser did.

"He couldn't do nuthin' 'bout it. What would you do? If you heard a couple arguing, you wouldn't automatically assume the guy she was speaking to was about to kill her."

I had to ask. I got up and walked to stand behind the hefty lady's chair and looked into her mirror to meet both women's eyes. "I didn't hear about that. What happened?"

"Oh, honey," the stylist continued. "This worker was throwing out the trash last Friday night and heard a man and a woman arguing. He couldn't remember everything they said, because at the time, he didn't want to be rude and eavesdrop. But later that woman was found dead and he came forward to tell the police what he saw."

I tried not to sigh, but she took too long with the details. "Did he see the guy?" I pictured Pitch and cleared my mind.

"Not too good, no," she answered and coifed her customer's hairdo with both hands. "He saw a tall woman leaning on the window of a white van and she was talking mean, you know, not shouting, but sounding mad. Then she backed away and he saw her face enough to know it was the lady they later found dead."

"She was trans," the Scot said from her chair.

"She was a *lady*," the stylist stressed and returned her eyes to Ruth's in the reflection. "Anyway, the boy said she didn't like the guy in the van and called him some bad words. The only thing he could remember for sure was he heard her say, 'I wouldn't go home with you if you were the last man on earth, you shithole.' And he scooted inside to joke about it with his friends."

I repeated the phrase in my head adding in the coincidence of the white work van at the Rakum church.

David Walker wouldn't let all this go on, right? Unless it's a sham, the whole caboodle. All the Rakum gathered together to commit murder between Bible studies?

None of that sat right with me so I returned to the woman calling the suspect a shithole.

Is it possible for a woman, trans or not, to reject Pitch?

I shook my head. Why was I so determined to make this about my patient? It could be any Rakum; I agreed with Keifer and Darcy on that. It was one of their brothers. But it didn't have to be Pitch. I thanked the women and casually left without a haircut.

Outside, my Northface jacket protected me from the wind and I rolled the high collar over my cheeks. I jogged for the next store, a Panera Bread café. Once I'd ordered a large coffee and a bagel, I found a quiet corner and turned my back on the world. Hunched over my phone, I nibbled my brunch and flipped through my email. When that grew old, I looked at my social media groups and sighed when nothing caught my attention. Once the tabs closed, I noticed a new message. I opened it and found a photo attached to a DM from a user I did not follow called, *Pitchforker.*

Pitch.

I flushed and didn't press "open." I hadn't seen nor spoken to him since inside the limo. Then, I added the sex tape he sent—so that was the last I saw of him, making love to Darcy Vandiver. I swallowed, remembered I was mad at Kiefer for everything, and opened the message.

"Hey, doc, put me down for tonight, 7pm. I've missed our sessions, spent the week checking on my shit in Mississippi. I'd like to bring you there—it's the sort of place women like. A giant house, empty except for me these days. Needs a woman's touch. So big and throbbing with untapped potential. Heh

By the way, you think I called you Ruthy to hurt you, but it just came out. You're so damn sensitive—if you'll take a word of advice from a new human, back off the victim shit. You survived. If someone calls you something you don't like, toughen the fuck up and carry on. You think I cry and fall apart every time I don't get what I want?

See you tonight. And I'm sorry I hurt your wittle feelings. If you'd only let me, I can make you forget all your troubles. -P

I read the message twice before tapping the photo thumbnail, which I could see was going to be his head. Enlarged, it was surprisingly normal—Pitch holding the camera away from his face for a selfie. He had taken care with the staging; his hair perfectly styled, chin tipped down with his eyes up and a very engaging smile on his lips. Suspicious, I examined the background, reverse-pinching and scanning the edges. Pitch stood in a bedroom, the bed large and coated with a silk or satin maroon comforter that reflected the light source. Nothing odd that I could see.

Finally, I let it resume its shape and I hit a return message.

"See you at 7," I typed and on a lark, I lifted my phone to eye level, opened the camera app to view my face, and I pointed with one finger in a *you behave* gesture. Once the shutter clicked, I looked good—my makeup and hair and the lighting at my table—I hit send.

Immediately, he returned a message.

"I'll use that to beat off, thanks, Doc."

I closed the app and set down my phone. But I wasn't mad. He had a point; why was I so sensitive if I was healed from those old wounds? Had I been playing the victim the whole time I called myself a survivor?

When my phone buzzed with Kiefer's assigned tone, I realized I was already smiling—at Pitch, not my lover.

"Where are you?" the text read and I gave my location and asked him to pick me up.

"I'll use that to beat off, thanks."

That Pitch. He keeps me on my toes.

The Sneak

Well, I got a new car.

When Keifer picked me up at Panera, the first thing out of my mouth was how he left me without transportation, which was mean and thoughtless and *yada, yada, yada*. Yes, I had morphed into a nagging bitch and my lover's resolution was to go from the café to a car dealership and buy me a brand-new Nissan Maxima. He tried to get me a Mercedes, but no thanks. I'll take a car as a gift because he's so rich, but I'll be damned if I'm going to let him pick the vehicle I'm supposed to drive every day. My old Maxima worked great, carried me safely and economically for four years. So for $32K, I drove away with a ruby red sporty sedan of my own choosing.

Right now, it's nearly seven and Kiefer is at the house, NOT going to church tonight or tomorrow. He said he's staying with me "a few days at least," and I'm going to soak that up as long as I can.

I sat at my desk waiting for Pitch and our 7 pm session, and when I lifted my phone to scroll some pages,

I received a new text from Jenny.

"LO AND BEHOLD! YOUR HOT BOYFRIEND IS SMOKIN' IN PERSON!"

It was to be a multi-part text as I watched the dots oscillate and she added more. Had she run into Keifer somewhere? Then a photo populated instead of a text. I blinked and looked hard before reverse-pinching in disbelief. Jenny and Keifer stood mostly center, his arm over her shoulders and hers about his waist. She was no taller than me and her cheek barely reached his pecs. This was surprising enough but behind them. Holy shit. Not part of her photo but clear as day, Pitch stood in conversation with Tiff over Jenny's right shoulder. I snatched up my landline handset and punched in her number.

"I knew that'd catch your attention!" she said when she answered. "Last night, after Tiff's reception. I left to visit the bathroom and ran right into your man!"

"Where? In Tuscaloosa?" I asked trying to determine their location by the background.

"No, in Hoover, at the Marriott—Tiff's team sponsored the Intramural Community College awards ceremony. Keifer said he was there at a conference of his own, and damn, whew! He is hot! And talk about sweet?" she added with a southern twang she normally hid. "He's so polite. Hold on to that one, honey."

I didn't smile at her jovial tone. Last night, after that wonderful romp, Keifer and I went to sleep. I wanted to say to my friend, *"last night?"* but she'd get wind of my suspicion and I didn't want to explain myself. Inside, I clicked off the time; we'd fallen asleep early, maybe 9:30. Tuscaloosa to Hoover, 50 miles.

My mouth said, "What time was that?" Jenny paused

and I grimaced and added to cover my question, "He stays busy, that's for sure!"

"It was nearing midnight when I saw him. Tiff and I were heading out. Hey, his friend—what's his story? Tiff said he was really, *really* interesting. Which means he was able to push through her man-hating barrier."

Jenny laughed at her words and my mind race with why? *Why would he sneak out? Why would he lie?*

Well, he hadn't lied, but he also hadn't come clean. He left the house when I was asleep, drove an hour away to a hotel with Pitch, and drove back in time for me to awake in his arms.

A hotel with Pitch!

KIEFER!

At the entrance to my building, the doorman buzzed someone in. I told Jenny I had a patient and she let me go. My mind raced with Keifer's deceit. Why lie? I got up and opened the office door so Pitch could just walk in and I dialed Kiefer's cell. I'm sick of the sneaking and lying and pretending and fake, fake, fake Jesus shit! I was fuming inside when he picked up.

"Yeah, baby?"

"Why did you go to Hoover last night after I was asleep? Did you need to fuck a brother so badly that you had to do it behind my back?!" I had spoken harshly and Pitch entered as I barked the last phrase.

"I wasn't fucking," he said as calm as ever. "What's going on?"

My chest heaved and Pitch walked to his usual chair without sitting. He met my eye and nodded in agreement with my lover. Deflated, I asked, "Then why did you go to that hotel after we went to bed?"

"I'll tell you one thing," he said, his voice carrying an

edge I didn't often hear. "I don't like being shouted at, and you can keep your inquisition. How much of this does a mortal man take?"

It had been a sincere question and guilt and regret speared my heart. Pitch stood staring at my face and Keifer also awaited some sort of something from me.

"I'm sorry, babe," I said contrite and calming down. "So much going on and I haven't been able to talk to you about any of it. I'm sorry." I looked at Pitch. "I'm sorry."

"I'll be home at least three days. Tomorrow's Saturday. Let's go on a trip. You and me and you can tell me all the things I've missed while away in Tuscaloosa."

I grinned and the happiest joy blossomed deep inside, an old joy, something I hadn't felt since I met Pitch and started down the current road to Helltown.

"Yes, let's. Yes, thank you. And I'm sorry again. You're doing great, babe. It's me—and getting mad right now? That was very human. You're awesome, you know?" I had turned my back on Pitch and spoke to Keifer facing my desk. He said he loved me and I ended the call.

It was Pitch time.

Pitch, Session 5, 7:00pm, Friday
True-Client Software™ **bolds Client's spoken word**
MedVR™ transcripts used to populate dialog, build entry
Loc: My office on 27th Ave

Notes: None

"Doc, doc, doc," Pitch *tsked* as I settled in my desk chair and he into his Queen Anne. **"I haven't fucked Keifer since that time last October. We coupled because it**

came naturally; I sprung it on you to get a reaction, but we were doing it because we like it. It wasn't to get at you."

I nodded, still in apology mode even though the session had started. Once again, I tossed my professionalism out the window for the Rakum, and maybe I always would to some extent.

"Why sneak off to Hoover?" I asked guessing he would tell me and he shrugged.

"I don't think he was sneaking. I think you fell asleep and he wanted to stay up. I have a card game in that hotel on Thursdays and he joined us. All brothers. No sex."

"Oh," I said in an exhale. Pitch sounded different, less edgy, or maybe it was my imagination. I was beginning to question things I had been taking for granted. "Why is your voice so soft?" I asked to avoid word games I'd normally play with clients.

"Soft?" he said, his brow raised. **"There's nothing soft over here, I assure you."**

Why did he have to be so handsome? I did not like the way I watched him so closely, studying and memorizing his lines. He chuckled with a blush (!!) when I didn't respond.

"It's probably that church shit," he said still chortling ot the side. **"I watched another sermon on the feed."** He shrugged. **"It might be dulling my knife a bit."**

Ugh. The church. I didn't want to discuss God. "Good enough," I answered. "Let's start the session. I have some new ideas."

"Go." Pitch crossed one leg over his knee and leaned back, elbows on the armrests.

"You were in your own house a week. Tell me how

107

you passed the time? Do you have brethren there? You said the house was empty except for you."

"You didn't see it, did you," he said as a statement and fished out his phone.

I gave him a blank look, inside, working to guess his meaning. He found a photo and turned the screen to me. It was his selfie, the one he sent me from his Columbus bedroom. With an attempt to seem disinterested, I found the image on my own phone and again, scanned the background. Nothing. He grinned and waited. I returned to the photo and sent it to my email. In another sixty seconds, I had it pulled up on my monitor and with my photo-editing software, I enlarged it to fill the 19" screen.

Pitch rose and crossed to my desk. Without a concern, he came around blocking me in because of the furniture configuration. He looked to the display and I gave him a tiny glance. Like always, he smelled delicious, and tonight wore a soft mint-green cashmere v-neck sweater over black jeans and boots. Also, as always, he wore no undershirt so his chest hair fluffed out and caught my attention if I dropped my staunch avoidance. I enlarged the photograph and used my cursor to examine the outer edges.

Then I saw it.

On the nightstand, nearly impossible to see on my phone screen, sat a sheet of typing paper. In the center was a familiar shape — my face and shoulders from my professional headshots. This one was used on my website. I looked to Pitch standing inches away and also looking at the computer screen.

"A print-out of me," I said watching his profile.

He smiled without looking over, his eyes to the image. He lifted a finger and touched the screen. I squinted my eyes and then used the program to further enlarge the area.

"Oh," I said very small. Pitch had typed a note above my photograph. In what could have been Times New Roman it read, *"People I'd like to Fuck,"* and the numeral one sat near my cheek. It wasn't shocking and I wasn't insulted. This wasn't new news. I looked back to his profile and he turned his face to mine.

"I'll never give up," he said close, his breath minty and his gorgeous eyes dancing about my face.

"It's not going to happen," I said soft and as kindly as possible. He exhaled, grinned anew and paced away to his seat. Once he had settled down, he launched into a story about his Mississippi house and its repairs.

He kept my photo beside his bed. So? I wasn't going to have sex with him. Ever. Even if he was the last man on earth.

Shit.

My mind had returned to the killer and the witness, the last one to see the Tuscaloosa woman alive. This was something Keifer and I could discuss while on our little trip. We'll get away from all of it.

I refocused and pictured a warm cabin in the woods where Keifer and I made love over and over and over, with no Darcy, Pitch or Jesus to interfere.

The Dreamer

ake Tom Bigbee rented the cutest cabins I'd ever seen and when I returned home from the session with Pitch, my lover had already packed our bags and his Jeep with all we'd need for two nights away. We filled our waking hours with eating, lovemaking and discussing everything in the world pertaining to our lives now and into the future. It was the closest thing to heaven I had ever experienced and when we returned home Monday noon, he kissed me and left for Tuscaloosa. That was a week ago. I didn't like it, but he made my weekend so wonderful that he'd bought some extra grace. Pitch cancelled his sessions and I didn't see him all week either. For a split second I wondered if they were together, but I quashed my unfounded suspicions. No, Pitch had probably gone home but I sure as hell wasn't going to text him to find out.

My phone dinged.

"I'll be home tonight. CUSoon."

We're gonna make it. He loves me… I smiled and hugged myself and sat in the recliner to wait.

I must have fallen hard asleep because I woke to the sensation of being cradled close and as I, by instinct, hugged my arms about his neck, I recognized Keifer's cologne. Without opening my eyes, I murmured a sleepy hello and he carried me to our room. Once there, he placed me carefully, as if I were made of glass, and I watched him shrug off his clothing, his silhouette just visible in the available light. I smiled and forced myself awake—he was nude and sliding into bed, facing me with his adorable let's-make-love posture.

By draping himself over me, his chest against my nightshirt, he said at my ear, "I missed you, baby." And he found my mouth, kissing me deeply, as if we'd been making out for hours. Usually, there's a build-up, but I played along, catching up as best as I could. He whispered something in his language—that was rare but not too strange—and I let it pass, since we'd been apart so long, I assumed he'd been simply hungry for my attention.

Then his uber-passionate kiss wasn't the only thing he rushed; unlike our normal routine, he used one hand to cup and gruffly squeeze my right breast through my shirt. His grasp did not release, but held and held and held, and when I was certain I'd have a bruise, I made a noise and his hand fell away, moving to my hair. He ran his fingers through it to the ends and then re-started only to fist it in his clutch at the scalp. Not hurting but immobilizing my head.

"Are you okay?" I asked just before he shoved his tongue into my mouth further than before, filling the space and not coming out. Gagged by the move, I didn't complain—how could I? He was starving for his Ruth.

My hands had been running along his back as far as I could reach in our current position and presently, he switched his hair-hand to keep his outside free and the one

111

pinned under my shoulders grabbed my hair at the scalp as before. He forced my head back to the pillow and moved his kiss to my throat.

Licking and sucking, he said in a whisper, "I'm going to fuck you, baby. You ready?"

I wasn't bothered by the treatment so far; although our lovemaking had never been so aggressive, it ran congruent with the sex his brethren delivered before their change. Maybe he was having a flashback experience. Maybe I needed to make mental notes for my Rakum Model. Maybe—

"Ow!" I yelped as my lover unceremoniously and without warning (or lubricant), shoved two thick fingers into my bottom. "What the fuck are you doing? Stop! Just stop!"

The fingers withdrew and he leaned propped up, his face without features in the dark. I cursed again, my ass sore and flashbacks of my own threatening to ruin our night, and I pushed away to hit the bedside lamp. My urgent clumsiness destabilized its base and, although the bulb switched on, the unit was knocked off the table taking its illumination to the floor. In that split-second glimpse of my lover, my eye caught a crown of black hair.

Pitch! Fuck!

I yelped and everything went dark. I was out.

When I opened my eyes, I was on the sofa facing the television. An old western was playing and I recognized John Wayne before I switched it off and sat up, looking about the dark room.

"Keifer?" I called and the quiet returned only that stillness empty places assume. Had I been dreaming? I scoured my memories. I had been waiting for Keifer, he came home, we started to make love and it wasn't Keifer. I'd only gotten a glimpse, but his hair was black...

PITCH!

I got to my feet clutching the throw blanket. I took one step and then another before my hand dropped to my panties. I swabbed the lining and a trace of something slippery moistened my fingertip. Next, I became aware of a soreness I hadn't felt in years. I carefully probed my backside and at that moment, Keifer walked through the front door.

"Hey," he said and then walked up in an urgent manner. "You okay? What's wrong?"

I clenched my jaw as I formulated my reply. *He's not a man. Not yet. I have to keep calm or he won't hear me. Be cool, Ruth. Be cool.* My internal mantra worked because I said, "I think Pitch was here. I think he raped me."

Standing twenty feet away, my lover's lips parted without speaking. Was he wondering how his favorite brother broke their trust? Keifer's pause had been less than a second, but I heard somewhere inside, *"or is he pondering who it was?..."*

Then he offered a cautious grin and took a step toward me and shook his head. "No, baby, that was me," he said catching my eye. "We had sex. When we finished, I stepped out for some air."

"No," I said and paused, thinking back. Elements of our lovemaking had differed, but not crazily. I only thought it was Pitch when I turned on the light. In my agitated state, could I have imagined seeing the devil instead of my Kiefer? And why did I pass out? I hadn't eaten or drank anything that he could have used to roofie me...

"I'm sorry, baby," he said then and stepped close, testing to see if I'd allow an embrace. I did and he pulled me to him, the newly detected aroma of his cologne chasing away my anxiety. "I was stove up," he added with a chuckle that sounded embarrassed—*which is an advancement,* my doctor-hat whispered.

I finally lifted both arms and hugged him back, my cheek flat against his strong chest.

"I don't like it that way, Keiff. I told you…" I whimpered the last phrase and hid my sudden tears. The shock of several different trespasses lined up in my mind, being probed and then sodomized while unconscious had occurred in my past, but never with Keifer – never with the man I hoped hold to the end of time.

"Come to bed, I'll fix it," he said low and kissed my forehead his gentle touch moving to encompass my neck. I met his gaze and his eyes said he loved me with his entire Rakum-human heart.

I was lost and fell back in love with him, the entire episode fading into oblivion. I gave him a tiny smile and he wiped my cheek with his strong fingers.

"Can I carry you?" he asked as if cognizant that I might resist (another good sign that he is adapting). I allowed it having already marginalized the situation. The light had been a flash and filled with shadows. I was disoriented by so many things that the harsh shadows caused by the incandescent light could have darkened his hair.

I mean, look at him; he loves me so much!

In an easy movement, I was in his arms and he took me down the hallway. I grinned when he comically avoided my head hitting the room threshold and again when he curled his arms to bring my face to his.

"I love you, Ruth Angleton," he said deep in my eyes. "I want you to be my wife—like a mortal wife. Not a mate.[5] Will you?"

My heart pounded and I squealed with joy, squeezing his neck, repeating, "Yes, yes, yes!" in his ear.

"Good," he said and lowered me to the floor. I hugged him again and turned for the bathroom.

"I'll be right out. Get in bed, handsome," I said and jogged inside the small room to clean up. My heart racing with anticipation of what the future may hold, I used the toilet and flushed.

When I stood, my eye fell to something on the floor that hadn't been visible from the toilet. It looked like a glove. My mind went to a conversation I'd had with Keifer at the start of winter. *"I hate gloves. In the old days, I got frostbite rather than wear anything on my hands..."*

I stepped to the object and touched it with my toe. It was definitely a black leather glove. When I had taken a deep breath, I stooped to pick it up. It was lined with white rabbit fur and the label poking through the beautiful down was bright orange.

Pitch's glove.

I broke into a sweat, dropped the glove into the trashcan, and covered my mouth with both hands. What had my lover done? And ... more... *why would he do it?*

I was only twelve. Was he really asking me to marry him?

"We'll have to wait until you're seventeen to get married for real, but we can have a private, secret marriage until then. Okay?"

Aaron had led me into the closet, the place the old ladies stored the choir robes. It smelled of dust, moth balls, and feet, but Aaron said it was a magical spot where the world didn't exist. There were no rules in here, no right and no wrong, just love. Pure love between a man and a woman. Aaron dropped to his knees facing me.

It was time to get married and I tried not to cry.

14

The Disappearance

In the light of day, I convinced myself that I'd been confused by the lighting, disoriented by my current mental worries. After kissing Keifer's cheek, I rolled out of bed and entered the bathroom. My caboose was still sore and might be for a few days. I never enjoyed that, but my past abusers had. El-A and his brothers had. When I sloughed off my Cow persona and adopted that of the survivor, I decided I would not engage in any sexual activity I did not enjoy. Last night better not happen again.

With a shiver at the memory, my eye fell to the corner where I'd found the glove. I had tossed it into the trash. Why? Shouldn't I take it to my session with Pitch? Even if it had been Kiefer in my bed (and I wasn't 100% certain yet), the glove indicated Pitch had been in my house. When and why?

Card parties…

I locked the bathroom door and turned on the shower.

Kiefer had two pastimes before he met Jesus. Taking long solo drives and visiting with his brothers. Before we moved in together, his brethren played cards at his place. I'd see them there sometimes when I slept over. Once we

117

bought this house, I never saw them here. I considered this a sign of our commitment to each other, that he wanted me for himself, holding me close. There were signs he had them over now and then, but it never gave me any concern.

I tested the water with outstretched fingers and slipped off my tank top.

Maybe that's it; Pitch dropped it when he was over here playing cards.

In our bedroom?

I gave that some thought and stepped under the jets. It wasn't outlandish if two men needed to go at the same time. If the downstairs bathroom was *occupado,* Pitch could have jogged upstairs to our room.

I sighed and commenced my shower. Keifer was here, he loves me, we're getting married. Maybe I could move this shitty memory to the "Closed" files and have a happy life. I pushed the whole thing aside and sang pop songs in the stall.

A few minutes later, I stood in front of the mirror to apply my makeup. In thirty minutes, I'd need to head to my office. I thought of Pitch. I would see him tonight for his 6th session and I hadn't seen him *(I hope)* since last week when he told me he'd never give up on getting me to bed. On a lark, I stepped to the trashcan and lifted the toe-activated lid.

Clean bag, no trash. The glove was gone.

Private Chat / BessemerMentalHealth.org (BMH)
Topic: **RAKUM SERIAL KILLER**
Thread title: **Patient07 Rape/Torture/Souvenir (tongue)**
Thread Owner: Ruth Angleton, PhD
Participants (in italics): Heather Flank, PhD/ Josh Klaus, RN

: Checking in. How did it go? Our guy hasn't made the news in seven days. Did you get through?

: ...

: Heather? Your avatar is on. Hello?

: *Dr. Angleton – it's Josh. Can I call you? Something's wrong and I could use some help.*

: Sure, sign off first.

Josh Klaus is Heather's lover. When her avatar blinked out, I logged off and looked at my phone. It rang before three seconds elapsed.

"Doc, Heather's missing." Josh's voice strained and his respirations caused me to imagine him shuffling papers and seeking clues. "I called the police when I got to her office. It's completely wrecked. I gave them her computer. Your number's on her corkboard. Please tell me you have some insight…"

I hadn't spoken or even *"Hmm-mm'd"*, too much in shock to respond. Patient 7 did this, and two questions looped in my mind: how much do I tell the authorities if they question me, and will Patient 7 come after me next?

"Doc? You there? Did you hear me?"

"Yeah, sorry, I'm just… give me a sec." I glanced at the time, closing in on 7 p.m. Pitch was due any moment. Then, I glanced at the door to my office—closed but not locked. I got up and shuffled across the room and turned the bolt.

"The police asked who you are to Heather. I told them everything I know."

"Good." I still didn't know what to say to the man. He knew nothing of the Rakum and I began formulating my spin for the cops. My cell phone vibrated in my hand and I made goodbyes to Josh, promising to call him back.

I looked at the screen. Keifer. He wanted me to know he had returned to Tuscaloosa. Shit! I was sick of that church! I need him here! The only other therapist who is helping his brothers is missing and maybe dead, and he's off dancing with Jesus! Keifer's obsession with God was tanking our relationship.

My desk phone buzzed and I yanked up the handset with one more glance at the clock. It was seven on the dot.

"Dr. Angleton? I'm Detective Paramus with the Corinth PD. Can you answer a couple of questions?"

The staccato voice of the cop helped me to focus and I told him to go ahead, but hurry because I was expecting a patient.

"When did you last see Heather Flank?"

"We don't see each other, Detective," I said and trained my eye to my closed office door. "I know her online. We chat online and discuss patients and treatments. But to answer your next question, I last chatted with her on Tuesday, February 4th."

"That's specific..."

I flicked my eye to the BMH excel sheet, double-checked the date of her last entry and sighed for the cop. "I'm looking at the log. Look, I need to hurry. What else can I tell you?"

The detective hummed as if purposefully irking me and then said, "I'll need to see transcripts of that chat, please.

I'll give you my fax number."

"Uh, no," I said with a *duh!* in my voice. *The audacity.* "This is a private chat and filled with private patient information. You'll need a warrant to see them and there's nothing to see, anyway. We talk about methods of treating anger, that's all."

"If there's nothing to see, then send me a copy of your last chat."

"No, and I gotta go. If there's nothing else?" My eyes checked the clock. Pitch was late.

"Tell me about Patient 7," he said and my eyes widened. No way did Heather write that down. No way. When I didn't answer, he added, "There's a message she left for Josh Klaus and it says, 'if anything happens to me, call Ruth. She'll need to know to watch out for PT7."

He had spelled it out and I forced a laugh. "Geez, Detective, that's not PT for patient. It's a code from our online book club. Geez."

The cop was quiet a moment and then disagreed. "No, she left an audio message saying 'PT7'. Watch out for our book club PT7? Dr. Angleton, please. Whatever you can tell us might help us find your friend."

I wanted to scream, *SHE ISN'T MY FRIEND!,* but that was rude and not completely true. I mean, we shared information and ideas and theories, but like I said, I'd never met her in person—nor Josh. We had an online relationship and now she was screwing up my life with her big (maybe dead) mouth.

I grumbled for the officer and lifted my latest novel off the shelf and opened it to page 7. "*Old Palms Are Best,* by Helen Frye, page 7. '*Dimitri slapped on a grin and hid the knife in his desk drawer. His lover didn't need to know about the incident and he wasn't going to tell her.*'" Clutching the cell between my cheek and shoulder, I fluttered the books pages for the detective to hear. "It's erotica, look into it. Page 7 is where we find out Dimitri's a killer. My patient is here."

I hung up and crossed to the door. I was normally respectful of law enforcement, but not tonight. Once I'd exhaled and refocused my zen, I jerked open the door. The lobby sat empty. It was five after; Pitch wasn't coming. With a new anger fueled by frustration on so many levels, I shut down the office and headed to the nearest bar. Some fucker better not hit on me because if he does, I'm not sure I'll say no.

(ping!)

The phone pinged twice before I climbed to the surface of my sleep-ocean and peeked at the screen. Pitch had sent me a video. I paused and allowed my mind to de-fuzz. Before coming home, I'd visited a bar, drank two strawberry daquiris, and drove home. No one hit on me which hurt my pride, but it was Wednesday night, for Christ's sake. I exhaled and with a low-grade headache pulsing behind my eye, I hit play.

The video opened from a handheld camera, likely his phone, because the angle revealed only his face and shoulders, with one arm extended. Pitch was looking into the lens, not the screen, which I know from experience means he would have to force himself to look at the tiny black dot above the display to give this effect.

"I'm bored as hell, Doc," he said looking right at me. *"I had a date. It didn't end well."* He sighed and blinked his eyes hard before returning focus to the camera lens. *"I wish I'd come to our session instead."*

He sounded melancholy in that new-Pitch tone. I sat up and leaned on my pillows.

122

"Kfir takes you for granted. I wouldn't. If you were mine, you'd never get rid of me. I'd follow you everywhere you went." He chuckled low and licked his lips. *"I know that's not a positive attribute, but, Doc,"* he said and his gaze grew more intense, *"I might be obsessed with you."*

Pitch rolled onto his back, bringing the phone camera with him. Now I looked upon him, as if propped atop his strong chest. The bed wasn't maroon, it was deep blue, which meant he was in his Bessemer apartment where I had seen him romance Man Mountain.

I wasn't mad. I wasn't anything. I was dead inside. Heather was missing—possibly a victim of Patient 7. Keifer deserted me *again*. And here was his caustic brother, lonely and sad.

Had he been in my bed? I decided to ask and didn't think about what I did next. I hit Pitch's number.

"Were you here last night? In my bed?" I asked when he answered the call.

Pitch laughed one chortle. "No, but I can get there very quickly. You finally giving up on my kind and gentle brother?"

"Did you loan your gloves out?" I asked ignoring his jibe.

"What are you wearing?" he whisper-hissed, ignoring me right back.

Fuck-it. I was in no mood to play.

"Do you know Heather Flank?"

"Cow therapist," Pitch returned. "No."

"You know her name?" I mumbled.

"From our website," he replied without emotion. "Are you wearing panties?"

I closed my eyes with a sigh. But... at least Pitch was thinking about me. What's Keifer thinking about? God?

123

"Doc," he said, his voice somber. "Do you make house calls?"

I made a sad smile alone in my room and looked to the dark ceiling. I didn't have confirmation that Heather's disappearance was related to Patient 7 and I let it drop. "What's wrong? You said a date went bad."

"She was inconsequential," he said in a short Dr. Evil impression. "Kfir went back to Tuscaloosa?"

"Yep."

"I was going to make you a little movie, but the bitch wouldn't play. It's not easy watching a woman's mouth say no."

I huffed, so many different emotions, good and bad, assaulting my sleepy brain. None of the Rakum liked to be rejected; I couldn't pin the killings on Pitch for this reason alone. I sighed for him to hear. "Why do you keep sending me videos? I thought by pretending I didn't see them, you'd lose interest."

"Nah, I send them for myself," he said without pause. "I like imagining you seeing them, touching yourself. For a very short moment in time, Pitch makes you really, *really,* happy. That's what I pretend, anyway." He laughed at the end, a sad sound. His honesty shone through and I sensed a soft side to the Rakum I had the most trouble with.

"I want to ask you a non-therapist question," I said aware I would never ask him in person or even in the light of day. He said, *go.* "Are you capable of *not* doing things to hurt me? I'm asking because maybe it's a defect you'll carry forever." I kept my tone even, but I truly wondered.

"I don't know. I'm an ass, always have been. It's not just you. My entire existence has been to bring misery to mortals." He chuckled. "Now I'm mortal and making *myself* miserable." He laughed bigger before again falling quiet. "I

124

went to another one of Kfir's meetings; David said that once the Maker is part of my life, I would immediately see the world differently, act differently…"

Pitch had taken on a vocal impersonation of the Rakum preacher which brought a grin. *They mimic each other so well…* That caused me to think again about who might have snuck into my bed. *(It was Keifer, Ruth. Stop it!)*

I commiserated with a soft humph. "I don't know what to think. Do you feel different?"

"Yeah…"

Pitch paused and I waited. It seemed he was growing introspective and I would allow him to explore it. My therapist hat rose to the forefront, but deep down, I realized Pitch had morphed into more than a patient. Was he a friend now? It didn't seem possible but … who cares? I'm exhausted. My Rakum model would record everything and I could sort the data later.

Pitch said in an even tone, "The Rakum I respect most is Darcy Vandiver and he believes it—the Bible stuff, the stuff Beth Rider wrote about." Pitch sighed. "He said the Maker is calling me and that I should listen." Pitch huffed once. "I listened at that fucking meeting and ever since, I'm definitely thinking about this shit a lot more."

Gooseflesh rose on my arms at his words. I said low, "Are you joining the church?"

"No," he responded with a forced laugh. "But I might become more like Kfir. You'd like that, right?"

I was quiet, not liking the way my inner spirit confirmed every word when it never occurred to me to take religion seriously.

"Kfir said I should ask Jesus to wipe my slate." Pitch scoffed on his end before continuing. "He said Jesus forgave him for his sins, the ones he committed two

125

hundred years ago and the ones he commits tonight and tomorrow."

How did that make sense? I asked Pitch to see what he'd say. He offered a soft chuckle.

"Darcy said it like this. Mortals used to burn animals on an altar to convince the Maker to forgive them. Later, the Maker put an infant inside a virgin, got inside that flesh, and was born a human. When He was grown, He made Himself a sacrifice for the sins of all mankind for all time."

"So, if Patient 7 is a Jesus follower, he can do these murders, ask forgiveness, and it's cleared off his record?" I wasn't thinking of Keifer, *per se,* but of the church Rakum. Any of them could be the killer. If God forgives, what's stopping them from doing whatever they want?

"You're asking the wrong guy. I only mentioned it because you brought it up. I want to talk about you naked. How 'bout it?"

I said no; Pitch's religious bent had given me a headache.

"Doc," he said then in a soft voice, "you're alone. I'm alone. Let's fuck."

"Do you know who's doing these killings?" I asked, no longer provoked by his flirtations.

"Maybe," he said and nothing more.

"Now and then, the evidence points to you," I said, emboldened by no proximity.

"Hah. Better look at all of us—me, Darcy, Keifer. Hell, any of us have what it takes to do these killings."

"Keifer? Please," I said. "May as well accuse David Walker."

"Ruth, quick!" he said, suddenly breathy. "Put your hand in your panties."

"Bye, Pitch," I said and disconnected the call.

malcontent

I lay back in bed and waited, phone in hand, for Pitch to respond. He hadn't after a couple of minutes, and I set the phone on the nightstand. Soon after that, I fell asleep. In my dreams, I gave Pitch what he asked for and I wasn't even sorry.

The Romantic

Twenty-four hours passed and still no news on Heather's whereabouts. Keifer had asked about her the night I found out, but then left (again) for Tuscaloosa. I'm not seeing him much at all and besides the one time Darcy took me to Keifer's apartment, he hasn't invited me back. Oh, yeah, add to that, Pitch didn't come to his session – that night or tonight. When 7 p.m. came and went, I gathered my purse for home. Now it's nearly 9 and I sent Keifer a text.

"I'm saving a kiss for you."

I sent it away and sighed. The house we bought together was only half alive when he was gone. How long was I supposed to tolerate his absence? I walked to the kitchen and the doorbell buzzed. I had only taken two steps when I heard a deep voice announce, "It's Darcy."

I opened the door and Keifer's gorgeous friend smiled at me, showing perfect white teeth.

"Kfir sent me. Needs something from his desk."

Darcy didn't move to enter and I noticed. With a smirk I said, "Tell me where it is, I'll get it for you."

Darcy's reaction was to arch his brow a millisecond and then chuckle. "Very funny." His shoulders moved toward me a fraction but he still awaited my invitation. I sighed and stepped out of the way, making a dramatic sweep with one hand.

I didn't remember him ever going into Keifer's den before, at least not while I was home (or conscious!), but Darcy gave me a courteous bow and headed straight there. I followed and once inside, he approached the desk and looked into the left-hand drawer.

"You've been here before?" I asked, weary of guessing and once again suspicious of Keifer.

"Sure," was all he said.

When he had what he sought he stood up, six-foot-six, the most perfect man on the planet. I didn't look at whatever he had in his hand; my eyes were on his breastbone, my mind picturing him shirtless, swaggering after Pitch with his pants open. My questions dissolved as he walked past. I inhaled, every time I've seen him, his cologne sent me to heaven. I was lonely, *utterly,* and growing indignant regarding my "boyfriend" and his other hobby. How long should I tolerate being ignored? Was I being selfish? I needed to speak to Jenny and made myself a mental reminder.

I hadn't moved and Darcy cleared his throat.

"I'm heading to Tuscaloosa. Want to come?"

Did I want to come? *Hell yeah.*

But wait.

I wanted Keifer to come home to me. This was getting ridiculous. I narrowed my eyes, ready to ask Darcy point-blank about the homemade pornos. I tempered my tone to show I was above it all, and asked, "Did you and Pitch make that sex tape for me?"

Darcy inhaled with a grin. "In the foyer?"

I nodded and he chuckled, the sight melting me from

the inside out. *Shit,* let him do anything he wants—just have him keep looking at me with those eyes.

Darcy grinned wider as if fondly recalling the event. His handsome face angled to mine. "He sent that to you?" I nodded awaiting his answer. Darcy shook his head with a *tsk.* "It's not for you. Pitch always records our dates. He's certain that very soon, I'll be off the market so he's making tapes to jerk off to when I'm gone."

I watched his eyes, processing and wondering if he could be believed. *What am I saying? Of course, I can believe him. They don't lie about sex...*

"Well, he sent it to me, all right, and I had to know if you are as sick and twisted as he is."

"Is it twisted?" he asked then, a genuine question in his eyes. "What part? Making the video or—"

"Sending it to me. He's provoking me, trying to get me upset."

"He came up to Tuscaloosa Monday. He usually sees you on Mondays, right?"

I nodded, my lips parted. But what should I say? He skipped our session to what, visit my lover? I asked Darcy and he shrugged.

"I was gone all day, but when I returned to the church, I saw him driving away. Kfir wasn't there so he could have left. I didn't care enough to ask."

Darcy had spoken in an apologetic tone which I appreciated. My eyes fell to his hands as I pondered what Pitch was up to. The tall Adonis held a closed file folder and a professional SLR digital camera that I didn't realize my lover owned.

"Keifer needs a camera?" I asked. "He has one on his phone..."

Darcy shrugged, his little-boy grin returning. "Didn't

130

ask, didn't care." He turned for the door. "Want to ride with me?"

I shook my head but walked close enough to touch his huge bicep. "Tell him I want him here. This is enough. And tell him to call me. He's not answering his phone."

Darcy nodded and pulled the flaps of his coat together. He made an exaggerated shiver and after tucking the camera in a pocket and the folder under his arm, he pulled on a pair of leather driving gloves.

Gloves!

I stepped close again and he raised his brow. "Yes?"

"Tell me the truth, okay?"

"Always."

I moistened my lips and maintained a calm voice. "A few days ago, Keifer came home in the middle of the night and wanted to make love. I couldn't see him because it was so dark, but he smelled right and sounded right..." I took a breath and Darcy was listening. "But he started loving me in a different way and when I turned on the lamp, I thought I saw Pitch in my bed instead of Keifer."

I paused this time because Darcy grinned to the side.

"I fainted and when I came-to and told Keifer, he swore it was only him, that he was stove-up and..." I grabbed my butt cheek. "He did it all-wrong."

Still with that smile, Darcy looked aside.

"What? Tell me? Was Keifer lying?"

Darcy chuckled with a widening grin. "Neither brother confided this to me, so I would be guessing."

"But your face—what is it?"

"Pitch, Kfir, Ivan, lots of my brethren tag-teamed mortals back in the day—"

"Tag-teamed?" I repeated, interrupting him.

He took a moment to choose another phrase. "*Stood*

in for each other—is that better?" My face must have read how appalled I was, for he added, "If they did this to you, so what? You're okay. No harm done."

Incredulous, I said, "Have you not learned anything about how women feel about this issue?"

"Sure, they'd be furious, but you're not like most women," he said as innocent as a lamb. I asked him for more. "Because you were a Cow, for one. If this happened to you, it was not a novel event. And because you're a doctor, a psychologist digging into our Rakum mindset. You can see much more than the average human. If they did this, they assumed you could handle it. I know I would."

My eyes narrowed, my mind racing on his assertions. This Rakum regarded me as a person they could abuse and humiliate *carte blanche* because of my past and vocation. I was floored. I gave Keifer a ton of grace during his transformation process, but I had assumed he knew I didn't want to be poked in the ass while I slept. What crazy person would think a woman wanted that? I shook my head in amazement. But the answer stood right before me—they weren't *persons*. Fourteen months ago, most of them were vampires, blood-sucking, murdering, rapist monsters.

Darcy stepped in and lifted one big hand to take my upper arm in a tender grip. "You're making a difference, Ruth. You're saving lives—ours and the humans we might have ended in our anger and disillusionment. Have you considered how incredibly brave you are? Think about it. Is there another woman on the planet who can go through what you have and still maintain her objectives much less, her sanity?"

"I don't..." I started and stopped. He was giving me

a huge compliment and he wasn't finished.

"Because of my status among the brethren, I'm socially connected with hundreds. This means I am privy to their secrets and their privately held opinions of how our transformation is going as a whole. Every Rakum I speak with has heard of how Ruth Angleton helps our brothers."

"Darcy…" I tried again and he shook his head, his feathery hair swaying at his chin.

"Over time, Kfir will continue to be a better mate. Pitch will learn to better control his impulses, but he will always be an asshole. Me? I'm going to keep growing into whatever the Maker wants me to become. But am I going to dream of fucking my brothers the past 300 years?"

Was that rhetorical? I let it alone and he continued with a friendly huff.

"The point is all of us are better humans because of your efforts."

"Do you really believe that stuff about do whatever you want, and God will forgive you?" I asked, truly curious.

"Yes, but over time, a son grows into his Father's image. The brethren at the church will eventually stop ending the mortals around them."

I did not like it explained this way either. Whoever was killing these women needed to be punished—if God wouldn't do it, we had electric chairs available.

I sighed. None of that was getting my man back.

"You and Keifer and God," I said meeting his mesmerizing gaze, "will he still want me when he's done at church?"

Darcy dropped his hand and the other palm came up and cupped my throat. He leaned down to peck the top of my head and he stepped for the door.

"If you love him and will share him with the Maker, then you will remain mated. Kfir is not looking for a replacement." He put his hand to the knob, and I remained where I stood. "After I stop by the church, I'm headed to Pitch in Columbus. Do you have a message for your favorite patient?"

"Hah," I said in a weak laugh. "Yeah. Tell him to text when he won't be at his session. It's a waste of time for me to wait for someone who doesn't show. Tell him to imagine he was me, bathing, dressing, driving to the office to sit in a chair and watch the clock. He can take it from there and work on his empathy."

Darcy offered a small nod and pulled open the door.

"And thank you," I told him. He waved his fingers over his shoulder and was gone.

♦

I treated myself to a late dinner of pizza and cheese sticks, binging vampire movies on cable TV. I fell asleep somewhere in the middle and awoke to a chime from my phone. Like Pavlov's dog, I flushed to my toes and hoped it was a new sex tape from Pitch.

"Don't send our vids to Kfir's mate," Darcy was saying as the film opened. I swallowed and paced my breathing—they were kissing, bare-chested and wearing jeans, standing in the center of a large, stark-white bathroom. A lavish glass-doored shower stall large enough for four filled the background.

"Is that a command, Master?" Pitch answered his lips brushing across the skin of Darcy's arm. My mind aged them both since I'd learned that a Rakum's birthdate determined seniority in issues outside of military matters.

Pitch claimed 1800 and Darcy 1710.

"What do you think?" Darcy fisted Pitch's hair and forced his head backward, swooping in to cover his neck with heavy open-mouthed kisses.

"How will you enforce it?" Pitch asked, his voice rumbling with testosterone. He had ceased exploration of his lover's body and concentrated on receiving pleasure.

Darcy stopped what he was doing, released Pitch's hair, and stepped back. With a question in his face, Pitch remained three long seconds before exhaling with a wide smile.

"You wouldn't," he said in a chuckle and closed the distance. He grasped both of Darcy's wrists to place the big man's palms to his upper chest. *"An ish-mikhan doesn't use sex as a weapon."*

Pitch sounded certain, but Darcy wriggled free and turned around. He reached the sink and leaned upon it to gaze in the mirror.

"Do not send our videos to Kfir's mate," he said, his sexy voice rumbling and somber. *"The end."*

Pitch huffed and came up behind him. The devil ran both hands up Darcy's beautiful back and then wrapped him up, pressing in, his cheek to Darcy's tanned skin.

"_____" he said in their language (I assume) and Darcy turned in his embrace. He cupped Pitch's face in huge hands and kissed his mouth, resuming the dance.

I watched without blinking as they removed each other's clothing while walking to the shower. Pitch set the temperature and flow at a panel in the wall and the video filled with the sound of rain. Then, it became a new show, both men loving each other as tenderly as I had ever seen in any circumstance and speaking their language when they made words. I did not look away until both were spent, still in the shower, and breathing hard holding each other front-to-front.

I watched and waited, the steam from the shower had not obscured a thing and I walked to my lonely bedroom holding the phone screen before me.

"All of this is so different now," Pitch said in a whisper and I found myself amazed and happy his electronic equipment picked up the words. *"It hurts when you go away."*

Darcy lifted his hand and placed an open palm to Pitch's sternum. *"Did I tell you how Elder Canaan broke my human heart last winter?"*

Pitch shook his head, looking up into Darcy's face, both still standing close in the shower stall, water off.

"It was before he transformed and that left him the very last one of us still intact."

"The Last Battle," Pitch said low.[6]

Settling on my bed, I nodded to no one. Keifer had told me the story as he knew it. In the end, Elder Canaan also morphed into a human and presumably lives a normal life hidden from the brothers. I was wondering where the guy is now when Pitch resumed the conversation with Darcy on the video.[7]

"Canaan favored you. This was well-known."

"He did. But at this last meeting, he rejected me. Utterly. And he forbid me from ever seeing him again. I nearly died of heartache."

Darcy's mournful tone brought tears to my eyes as I listened on. Pitch was nodding with compassion and when I noticed, my doctor-hat made a note for my Rakum model.

"Since then, I've learned for mortals this pain is normal. It is emotional pain they endure their entire lives. Pain that comes from caring—we didn't have that before. Now listen to me, brother. Are you listening?"

"Go ahead," Pitch replied, his hands coming up to stroke Darcy's outer arm on either side.

"Let Ruth help you and stop getting in the way of yourself with this Rakum remnant lurking inside. If you want to live a long and healthy life, let her help you. Let Kfir tell you about the Maker. Listen and it will eventually sink in. Will you do this?"

I watched Pitch's grin lift on one side. *"Will you come by now and then and show me your magic?"*

Darcy leaned down and pressed a long kiss to his mouth. My chest constricted with worry for them, individually and as a people. Darcy had said it—they never felt such pain that I've endured since my birth. This meant he was right; I am stronger than I thought. Also, I'm stronger than the Rakum I treated. And the last thing he was right about, I need to keep at it. Keep teaching them how to love, because that will be their salvation; only by loving others would they learn to love themselves and cherish life.

My forehead prickled with a new thought—I was picturing Pitch in these observations, not the entire Rakum race, not Keifer, not my patients... The most dreadful Rakum I'd ever met had captured my sympathy.

Without warning, the video went black and I sat up on my mattress. When it flickered back to life, the couple had moved to a bedroom. The centerpiece of the gigantic space featured a king-size bed draped with a luxurious shiny satin maroon comforter with contrasting shams on the many pillows. The crown molding must have been twelve inches thick surrounding the ceiling, but then I recalled Keifer said his home was a restored plantation house, so the architecture and design fell right into place.

"Sleep over," Pitch said, shrugging on boxer briefs from the drawers of an enormous antique armoire. *"One last time.*

137

(then some words in their language)."

"I like my own bed, you know that," the big man answered pulling on jeans and watching Pitch climb beneath a luscious comforter. *"And why is it one last time? I have made no announcement."*

"Polsc-v'," Pitch replied.

My ears perked at the pet name Pitch had described after seeing Keifer's church and I watched to see if Darcy would melt his resolve at the sound. I had to smirk as without a verbal response, Darcy crawled onto the mattress. When he reached Pitch's tucked form, he dropped down, lying alongside on top of the covers.

"Go to sleep, brother. I'll stay until you fall asleep."

Lying on his back, arms up and behind his head, Pitch looked into Darcy's face. "(something in their language)."

"Be careful," Darcy said almost too low for the mic. I upped the volume. *"It's risky. You don't have to—"*

"Loltz, Darss," Pitch hissed, his interruption beginning with the Rakum word for shut-up, which I learned from my time with El-A Then, he spoke low in their language several sentences before Darcy shed his jeans and shimmied under the covers. He hugged himself behind Pitch who rolled to his side to spoon. Both men made settling-in sounds and fell quiet. I watched the quiet duo until the lamp clicked off.

He didn't have to what? What was risky? Was he hushed because of the camera? And if so, was he shushed because I might see it? I allowed my mind to hop down rabbit holes of possibility, many of them pointing to the topic of Patient 7. I often felt Darcy and Pitch knew more about the guy's identity than they let on. As if they had some names in mind but were not willing to discuss with me, a mortal. And a woman.

"Stay with me, be my mate," Pitch said then in the darkness, his humble tone causing me to think he forgot the camera. *"I could be harmless, I could accept it, I could—"*

"Shhh, my beautiful, beautiful man," Darcy replied in an affectionate rumble, cutting off his words.

I could be harmless… What was Pitch saying?

"You're upsetting yourself," Darcy said low.

"Have you even imagined it? For me, for our history, allow a brain cell to imagine us as a couple. Fuck, you owe me that much." Still with the begging voice, Pitch awaited a response.

In vain I wished I could see them, but only the edges of the window were visible. Why hadn't Pitch used a night-vision camera? My frustration aside, I imagined them as they were when the room fell dark and waited to see what Darcy would say.

"Go ahead, baby," Darcy said low. *"Tell me what you see."*

Pitch exhaled and began with a frustrated growl. *"You and me? The sky's the limit. Your looks and my brains? We'll insinuate ourselves into every elite mortal clique; fuck, we'll own the entertainment industry, tell those puppets what to do and say. Get sucked off by starlets. It'll be fun. And imagine us arriving together to the President's parties—to the mortal world, we'll seem the most famous couple alive—arm in arm in tailor-made tuxedos. And the courtesans…"*

Darcy huffed a laugh. *"Courtesans?"*

"You'll need them, polz̧. You'll wear me out in a year if we don't have backups," Pitch said with a sad laugh. *"And I'll move to Atlanta, we'll set up house together. Can you see any of this?"*

Darcy did not answer with words and I wished again for more light as I heard them kissing. It was a full minute before one of them spoke.

"I can see it, baby," Darcy said, his voice kind, *"but it's not for me. Can I tell you why or are you closing off?"*

139

The lamp came on and Pitch fell onto the mattress, on his back, looking at the ceiling. Darcy was on his side, propped and looking upon Pitch's face.

"I'm listening," Pitch muttered.

"I've been alive 309 years and have lain with my brethren more than 200,000 times—and that count is from before 11/13."

Pitch exhaled and draped one palm over both eyes as Darcy continued.

"It's fun and easy, but it's old." Darcy lay his hand flat to Pitch's chest, the covers pushed to his middle. *"The Old Way is old to me—all of it. I want something new. It will make me new again. Soon, I will begin my search for a female life-mate and when she is found, I will never fuck my brothers again."*

"I know, you told me, but..." Pitch dropped his hand and turned his head to meet Darcy's eye. *"I hoped you'd get over it, this crazy notion to dump your past."*

Darcy shook his head. *"This is the new Darcy Vandiver. Like all Rakum, I still want what I want when I want it, only now, I want something different."*

"I think David Walker is doing this to you," Pitch replied reading Darcy's face.

Darcy sighed and collapsed onto his back. He flicked his eye a millisecond to the camera as if just remembering it was on. *"I'm done talking,"* Darcy said and closed his eyes. *"Kiss me, blow me, or go to sleep."*

Pitch lifted to click off the lamp and his shape moved atop Darcy. I listened, breathless, to them re-starting their engines. With a careful exhale, as if someone might hear me in the deserted house, my finger headed for the stop button. Then Darcy spoke, his rumbling voice gentle.

"You're going to send our vid to Ruth. I'm not an idiot..."

"I know you're not," Pitch replied. *"Feel this, kilscz,[8] and shut up."*

140

I watched the edges of the window, the light of the moon seeping in and just as the recording reached the last second, Pitch's voice said in a conversational tone, *"Thank you for watching, Princess."*

I gasped and turned off the feed.

♦

It was four a.m. when I next opened my eyes and in less than a second, the most recent sex vid came to mind. I sat up and turned my face to the curtained window, as in my mind, Pitch kissed Darcy's jaw and led him to the shower. I no longer thought of Kiefer upon waking, my subconscious changing channels for its own self-preservation. It doesn't mean we're over, but a cursor in the back of my mind started down that road, scouting out life without my lover. For now, it would blink in the background, but I did not make it stop.

What was Darcy talking about and Pitch hushed him? I clicked on the bedside lamp and sat up, putting my feet to the floor. Rubbing my eyes with one hand, I reached for my cell with the other.

It's time I tested Pitch the way he tests me.

Without planning nor using any energy to consider my appearance, I turned on the video app and reversed the lens to my face.

"Wake up, Pitch," I said when the timer indicated the recording. "What was Darcy talking about when he told you to be quiet, that it was risky?"

I sucked my teeth, noting my sour morning mouth. I hadn't brushed my hair. But a Rakum wouldn't care, he wouldn't even notice. If I taught myself one thing this past month was that they are not near as human as I gave them credit for. Maybe they never would be.

"Then you said that you could be harmless," I added and tilted my head, studying my face in the camera. I looked at the screen and licked my lips. Then I stared into the lens and said, "Explain this to me or get out of my life." I held my eye in the tiny black iris. "Sometimes, you're amazing, but I'm tired of playing your game."

I pressed the stop button and lowered the phone. I played the video twice and sent it to Pitch. If he gave me the truth, I'd move him out of the trash heap. If he didn't, I meant what I said. I am tired of wrestling these Rakum. I was still in the same position, sitting on the edge of the mattress leaning over my lap when my phone rang.

Pitch.

"Hey," I said low.

"Bossy, bossy," he said with humor in his voice. "Don't you ever sleep? The bats are still out, you know."

Weary as I was, that made me grin, thinking of cute little bats fluttering around outside. I had always thought those were fun to watch. I allowed a friendly huff and nothing more.

"You think it's about you? Or your investigation?" he asked.

My lips parted to answer, and I stopped. No. More. Games. I remained silent and counted the seconds.

"Sh-i-i-i-i-i-t," he hissed with a comical warble. "It's sort of about you. It could hurt your wittle feelings, though, that's why I don't just say it. My therapist wants me to try to be human." He cleared his throat and part of me wished we were in the same room.

Ruth, stop that...

"It's okay. Tell me." I rolled in my lips, unable to guess what he might say. I couldn't even prepare myself, so I

142

hoped for the best.

"The context was that Darss didn't want me to send you our vids anymore. I joked…" Pitch paused and said again, "JOKED," as if he had cupped the speaker to talk. "…That I would put a camera in your bedroom, there at your house."

"Oh, God!" I said and stood, my eyes skirting the room in jerks.

"I was joking, Princess, shit. Chill." Pitch chuckled on his end and then fell quiet. "I was trying to get a rise out of Darss, that's all. Think about it. It worked, right? Run that video again and you'll see."

I swallowed and processed his explanation. He offered a new tidbit in a neutral voice.

"If it helps your Rakum research, Keifer introduced me to the fun of hidden video cameras."

"Wait. What?" I said looking around the room again, this time closer and walking the perimeter.

"Sure, ask him about it when you see him next. That apartment he had when you met? Cameras." He paused and then said softly, "I know because I helped set them. Relax. He never sent me a video of you."

I pulled the phone from my cheek. Never in my wildest imagination would I have suspected Keifer of secretly filming us in bed. What if he had? What if he still did? I would not allow my past abusers to surface, but they tickled the back of my memory as I began my search.

"Are you looking for a camera?" Pitch asked and I didn't answer. I held the phone with one hand and turned items around on various room surfaces with the other. "Let me come over. I'll help you look."

I ignored him and flipped a stuffed bear Keifer won for me at a carnival.

"Better yet, let's hang up and you make me a new video with your phone, but this time, lie down and point it to your tits. Yeah, I'd like that."

I barely heard him. I set the phone down, hitting the red hang-up circle at the same time, and used both hands to search. If Keifer had hidden a camera, I was going to find it. My nerves jangled, but I had to admit I was happy with Pitch's response to my warning video. He passed the test. Yay.

16

The Detective

I agreed to meet the detective at my office because I sure didn't want him at my house. It was Saturday and I hadn't heard from Keifer—no calls, no texts, no nothing. And I did not find any hidden cameras in my bedroom, thank God.

Last night's video of Pitch and Darcy stuck with me more than the others and their every word circled my mind throughout the day. I'm discovering that my most horrible patient has a very soft side. How do I draw that out? And he had been helpful when I called this morning in the wee hours. *Helpful.* My mind was solving Pitch's problems when the gruff lawman tromped into my space.

"Heather Flank has been found." With an authoritative chest noise, Detective Paramus dropped a stack of 8" x 10" glossy photographs on my tidy desktop, as if we were performing a scene from *Law & Order.*

Dammit! Poor Heather!

I hardened my exterior for the cop, and maybe for myself. I spent a lot of time pretending to have no emotions, and when a personal acquaintance—and we had common goals—is murdered, I should allow myself to have feelings. I'm sure that's the advice Jenny would give.

"Dr. Angleton, I want you to look at this timeline, these photos, and consider how much you could help these women's families find peace."

My face was to the desktop where the stack of murder victim pictures lay, but I was looking at the corner of the top photo.

Timeline...

I had been keeping a timeline of my own. It showed incidences where Pitch could have been in the same location as the women were killed. The Tuscaloosa one had me freaking the most because Pitch missed his session the night her body was found only hours dead. Heather went missing after my 5th session, where Pitch spent the hour discussing first, my photo he jerked off to, and then his Mississippi home repairs. I went to the lake with Keifer and maybe Pitch went to kill Heather.

I kept sticking Pitch in the blank and part of me screamed for me to stop. It isn't Pitch.

But wait... Heather isn't transgendered.

The detective was saying the same thing and I returned my attention to his monologue.

"The F.B.I. says, and we agree, that Flank was killed by a copycat. This is why we're investigating her alone, while the Feds take over the others."

I flipped to the second and third photographs, still not looking at the poor, murdered women represented in them. The fourth was Heather and I rose from my bent over posture and met the cop's eye.

"I don't know how I can help you. Heather and I treat anger issues and emotionally dysfunctional patients. My name was on her corkboard. So what? How can I help? I wouldn't give you access to my patients and I don't have access to hers."

"But you have the chat log. If you give us the chat log, we can scour it for suspects. You do want us to find this guy, right?"

"Of course, but nothing in our chats is specific. Anyway, I'm not giving it to you. Get a warrant, and even then, I'll have my lawyer block it. Here."

I fished in my top drawer and pulled out a business card. Years ago when still working under Jenny, she shared her attorney with me when I set up my business license. He had a huge firm and handled just about anything a person in the mental health profession could come upon. The detective took the card, read the front, and tucked it into his notebook.

"You couldn't get a warrant, could you?" I asked, and his expression darkened.

"We might get one with this new evidence." He pulled a cellophane-wrapped item from his pocket and placed it on my desk. The evidence bag had been labeled, "H.Flank, foyer, pink silica, Bessemer, Lowe Heights Construction."

I pressed the stone with one finger, my mind going over the implications. My office complex was sought after by young professionals in a certain tax bracket, and one of the little things that made us so lovely was the landscaping. Under every perfectly manicured bush and tree, all maintained by a contracted lawn service, the landlord had placed natural river pebbles, all tinted pink. With an exhale, I put it together; someone from my building had maybe walked through Heather's foyer. Still, wasn't that also iffy? I tracked these home all the time. *Hell, I sweep them up twice a month in my own entryway, for shit's sake!*

I pushed the bag toward the detective and gave him a smile. "If you do, let me know. Otherwise, I don't see how I can help you. We don't see the same patients. There's no reason for my patients to be compromised because you find a pink rock in her foyer."

The cop tucked the bag into a coat pocket and re-packaged his photographs. Then he pulled on his gloves and situated an old-school fedora on his head. "Good day, Doctor. Call if you think of anything that might help us."

"Okay, and you call my lawyer if you get that warrant."

He left without a reply and I dialed the lawyer myself. Once I reintroduced myself and left my story with his receptionist, I hung up and sank into my desk chair.

Pitch didn't do this. I'm sticking him in because he's the easiest to finger. Who else can I put in those shoes? Who knows Heather?

Her first Rakum patient knows her. Patient 6.

And Patient 7. He never came into the office…

But he left a voice message!

My eyes widened as I recalled a file Heather sent when the patient first called and left a recording of his voice. I opened the BMH chatroom on my desktop and scrolled to the correct spot.

Private Chat / BessemerMentalHealth.org (BMH)
Topic: **NEW PATIENT / SHOULD I ACCEPT?**
Thread title: **Patient07 / Refuses to be seen in person**
Thread Owner: Ruth Angleton, PhD
Participants (in italics): Heather Flank, PhD
(mp3.attached, audio only)

: Did you listen? What do you think?

I pressed the speaker icon on the file and listened. The man's voice was higher than Pitch's, yet familiar. It kinda sounded like Kiefer when he's in a hurry. I focused on the entire message and then played it again for inflection and tone. Patient 07 said he'd heard of Heather from a brother and sought her advice on how to assimilate. Then he was gone. I returned to the transcript for a refresher.

: I think you should accept. At least do an ev. I wonder who it is. Have any ideas?

: Not a clue. I guess I'll accept. Hell, the last one turned out okay.

: Good. Log off and call him now. Those guys are extremely impatient, as you know.

: Okay, I just needed a little nudge. It got a little hairy with Patient 6 toward the end. Made me gun shy, I guess.

A lightbulb came on in my mind—Heather's Patient 6 was named Jarret. One of Keifer's church pals was named Jarret.

Duh! Ruth!

He'd been standing with David Walker, Ivan, and the others in Keifer's photograph. I recalled his face. He was Keifer's height with reddish brown hair and smooth cheeks. He'd been handsome in a dark way—but many of them were. The dots tried to connect in my head, but I returned to finish the re-read of my transcript.

: What? You didn't tell me anything bad happened.

: I didn't think it was important. He missed a session and when I nudged him about it, he threatened me. Just the once, but it got me spooked for a few days.

: How did he threaten you?

: I had called in at our appointed time and when he picked up, I opened by telling him he shouldn't blow off our sessions. That he should call or text if he can't make it so I don't waste my time. He blew his stack. In the space of a moment, he began ranting at the top of his lungs that I should learn when to shut up, that I talked too much and if he ever got the chance, he'd cut out my witch's tongue and eat it on the full moon...

I stood up from my desk and looked at my door. It was closed, but was it locked? I stepped over and checked.

So, the killer... was it Jarret? Calling in as a new patient? But if so, why? Did he make good on his threat to silence his doctor? And if it was him, why did he kill the other women?

My mind turned to the one who used to help me with this stuff. Keifer could help, could possibly solve the whole thing if he'd only lend me a fraction of the attention he gave God and David Walker.

I frowned and pressed Keifer's number on my phone. It rang once and went to voicemail. With an angry huff, I dialed Pitch, maybe in spite. The mischievous devil picked up on the first ring.

"Missing me, Doc? I'm touched," Pitch offered in lieu of a greeting.

"Are you in town?" I asked and looked at my watch. It was nearing four and getting dark with winter storms heading in.

"I'm in Columbus. Why?"

"Shit," I mumbled and he heard it.

"Come on, Doc. Stop resisting. Drive over. I'll put you up a few days and when Keifer notices you're gone, he can try to win you back." He made a sexual noise and added, "Of course, you'll be hooked on Pitch by then. But the game will be fun."

I disconnected and considered my options. On the computer monitor, the chat room feed had another page to go so I scrolled to the next line.

: But you graduated him, so I guess he was playing the mean yard dog to see if you'd drop him. My last two did that a few times before graduating. They want us to quit on them so they can tell their brothers it's not their fault.

: *LOL, that's what I told him later and he agreed. Anyway, I'll log off. Gotta call Patient 7 and set up an eval. TTYL.*

(end)

I had an idea to search our chats regarding Patient 6 — *Jarret*. With a backwards scroll, I found the first mention of him and opened the thread. Jarret had enrolled in her sessions a short five weeks after their communal transformation from vampire to human on November 13, 2018. He had been her first Rakum patient but earned the number 6 because she had treated five Cows before a Rakum ever showed up. I let it run.

Topic: **MY FIRST RKM/HE'S AMAZING**
Thread title: **Patient06/Good Start**
Thread Owner: Ruth Angleton, PhD
Participants (in italics): Heather Flank, PhD

: He's gone. I had to hop on right away and tell you how it went. You there?

: Yep, go ahead. Sounds like it turned out okay.

: Well, it did, really. I gave him the line Keifer said would help and although he didn't admit what it was I said, he smiled and said he knows Keifer from the Old Days.

I had to stop. Never had I questioned Keifer's helpful suggestions, but now? What was he having us say? I opened my files on my own Rakum patients and sought the phrase Keifer typed for me in their language. Without a care and deep down trusting Pitch more than Keifer for the moment, I took a screenshot with my phone and texted it to Pitch. I added, *"What does this say, please."*

My phone rang before a minute was up.

"Doll-face, this is from Kfir, eh?" he asked and I covered my eyes with weariness.

"Yes, please, no games. What does it say?"

"Why do you have it? Give me the context and I'll consider a reply." His voice was playful, but I sensed he meant it.

"Whenever me or Heather had a new Rakum patient, Kiefer said if we say this to them, that it would help. He said it was encouraging them to give us a chance and to contact him if they need any Rakum help."

Pitch chuckled into the phone, his deep voice sexy even though he was being shitty to make me wait.

"Oh, I guess it says that, too." He paused and made a little humming noise.

"Well? What else does it say?" I wondered if I wanted to know. Why had my hackles gone up about my beloved this past little while? Was it because he's always otherwise directed?

"I want something in return," Pitch said.

"What?" I mumbled, my eyes still covered. "Just hurry up."

"Tonight, when you go to bed, text me a photo of your thighs. Bare thighs. Is that too much to ask?"

I growled, and I'd never do that. But... "Okay, fine. What is Keifer saying to my patients?"

"He used some of our favorite sentiments, ones mortals hate. You sure you want to know?"

I dropped my hand and stared at the words on my screen. It was eleven words. Ninety-two characters. How provocative could it be? Exasperated, I asked him to proceed.

"There are two main translations. Want them both?"

"Pitch..." I grumbled.

"Want the nice one, first?"

"Never mind!" I said, ready to hang up, but then he began in a gameshow voice.

"She's a doctor and used to be a Cow. Smile and nod. I'm on the website."

I shook my head. "Okay. What am I missing?"

Pitch chuckled. "This is what it says in context. Call her Doctor, but she's just a Cow. To her face, smile and nod, but picture her nude, fucking your entire pack at once. I'm on the website—" Pitch stopped short.

"What?"

"Kfir's an asshole, you know…"

That tone was new and my ears perked. "I'm on the website what? What's the big deal?"

He continued in his normal voice, the humor erased. "I'm on the website, basically for either."

My stomach turned. "Keifer was telling them degrade her all you want because that's all she deserves, and if you fuck her, call me." I had replied in a whisper.

Pitch responded with a small affirmative noise. At least he wasn't being cruel.

"Okay, I'm in the middle of something. Thanks," I said and hung up. A Rakum wouldn't be offended by that behavior, maybe Pitch would just return to whatever he was doing before. I refreshed the chatroom and continued reading, my mind scowling that my lover would have us say such a thing to his brethren. My phone chimed and I read a new text from Pitch.

"Keep in mind that a Rkm who's never seen a therapist would see this as an encouragement. A welcoming thing, making him feel hopeful. It also tells the brother that Kfir already did it and he came out better off. Keep your perspective."

"Did he say this to get you to come see me for therapy?" I texted back.

"No, he showed me your website. That was all I needed. Don't forget my picture. I'll be waiting, cock in hand."

malcontent

I huffed and set down the phone. But I wasn't mad. Not in the least.

: I gave him the line Keifer said would help and although he didn't admit what it was I said, he smiled and said he knows Keifer from the Old Days.

: Good.

: The initial eval revealed he would respond to our model and he did. He answered my questions and besides an aversion to lesbians (a funny story), everything is going to be easy to address.

: Lesbians?

: Well, transgendered, too. Now that he's mortal, several women have turned him down and upon deeper inquiry, he would discover they were lesbian or trans. He asked me why a transwoman would turn him down — "don't they like men?" — but he didn't like my reply.

: You told him not to put mortals—any of us—in a box?

: That's right.

: Good. How does he handle it when he hears no?

: He wouldn't say, but his body language indicated that he became infuriated. I can't be sure, but a few of his remarks made me think he raped a couple of these women.

: Geez. Well, what else?

: Other than not liking it when women turn him down for sex, he's going to be great. I'm going to iron out all his other issues and tackle that one last.

Now I was mad again at Keifer. The asshole should be here helping me with this.

For god's sake, he knows Jarret!

He could give me insight. I lifted my phone and looked at my recent texts.

Darcy.

I hit the call button and he picked up after a few rings.

"You got Darcy," he said, always sounding as if he was smiling.

"You in town?" I asked and prepared for the no. To my amazement, he answered in the affirmative. "Can you come to my office? I could really use your help and Keifer is nowhere to be found."

"My help with what?" he asked, and it sounded as if he was walking, the background noise included a car horn.

"Keifer used to help me with this, but a detective came by asking about the killer. He seems to think the person who killed my friend Heather is involved with me, too. When I started investigating my chats with her, I found evidence that Keifer knows her patients. I need a trustworthy Rakum to help me out." I know I sounded exasperated at the end, but so what?

"Trustworthy, eh? That's a nice compliment," he replied, and the sound of a car door whumping shut occurred in the pause. "I'm in Birmingham so give me a half-hour."

I said I would and hung up.

Darcy Vandiver.

He'd help me sort it out and I'd do my best to forget I've seen him naked.

17

The Confidante

I buzzed Darcy in myself since our doorman had gone for the day. He came in my office looking as amazing as always, this time in a soft white sweater layered over a navy turtleneck, paired with dark blue jeans. How did he maintain that look? It was crazy how I hadn't yet grown tired of his amazing build, when my own man is just as handsome in his own way. At any rate, he and I sat in the waiting room instead of my office, him choosing the larger of my two couches.

"I appreciate you coming by," I said, and he shot me a grin. He said nothing so I dove in. "My friend Heather Flank was murdered. Like me, she used to be a Cow, and also like me, she treats the Rakum with their anger issues."

"I've heard of her," Darcy said and hushed again.

"She helps me—*helped me*—with my Rakum model. Her first Rakum client was named Jarret. Am I correct to assume that's the same Jarret from the church?"

Darcy offered a regal nod. I waited a moment and his expression remained static. I continued, assuming I could ask pointed questions at the end.

"Okay, a police detective is investigating Heather's murder and he turned his eye on me. Seems she had written my name on her corkboard and left a cryptic message for me to her boyfriend's voicemail. I made some shit up and sent him away, but then I read our old chats about Jarret and Patient 7, and found some things you can help me with."

"Do you still think Pitch is Patient 7?" he asked in a protective tone. I said no, and I meant it. "Good," Darcy said and waited for more.

"Listen. Jarret graduated Heather's program with flying colors, but I saw two red flags. One, he was furious at being rejected by lesbians and transwomen, and two, he once threatened Heather saying to shut her up, he'd cut out her tongue and eat it. The coincidence of that threat with the murders is too much for me to ignore."

"I understand," Darcy said and again, said no more.

I paused; was he going to be any help? So far, he was an ear, but I needed his Rakum brain. I tried another tactic.

"You've seen Jarret in recent weeks. Could he be killing these women? Maybe abducting Heather, too?"

Darcy inhaled and leaned back, kicking his long legs out to cross his ankles. "I'm not sure what Kfir does to help you with these things, but if I had a notion to ask Jarret about this and he answered in the affirmative, I'd never tell one of your people. What can I do to help you aside from blowing in my brethren?"

I stared at him and worked on my next question. He had a point; all the work Keifer and I did together was to help Rakum find inner peace. Keifer wouldn't "blow them in" either and I knew it. I sighed folded my hands in my lap.

"I wasn't thinking. I always told Heather that wasn't our business. We understand that your brothers are letting us help because we don't judge you for anything you might do while you're assimilating." I offered a truce apology. "I got carried away with the mystery. I'm also wondering if I'm safe. I also treat the Rakum. Was she targeted because she was a therapist? She's the only victim so far that wasn't trans." I pursed my lips. "I don't guess I've done anything to anger him."

He exhaled before responding and I discerned he was choosing his words. He drew one palm over his mouth and said, "The vestige of Rakum behavior that most manifests in my personality is apathy. I am interested in what affects me. The end. If Pitch or Kfir or maybe one or two of the others were in peril, I might pay attention and help. But for the most part, I'm interested in fulfilling myself alone. We are concerned for each other as a whole, but I don't pay attention to individuals until they do something to cross my radar. Do you understand what I am trying to say?"

"I think you're saying you don't care who's killing these women and you're not likely to start caring just because I asked for help."

He gave me an apologetic nod and glanced at the wall clock. I wasn't ready to release him.

"Okay, let me ask for a specific favor. You can say yes or no, but it's going to be good for your transformation if you say yes."

Darcy's lips formed a reflexive grin; I had hit a nerve because he prided himself on his assimilation. "Let's hear it."

"Will you feel out your brothers, Jarret, Ivan, Rusp, any of those at church or in the world or on your website, and make sure Dr. Ruth Angleton isn't on anyone's hitlist?"

With one more slow nod, Darcy rose to his feet. "I will put out the word you are protected." He fished for his phone and typed with both thumbs. He showed me the screen, but it was in their language. He dropped it back into his slacks. "The ish-mikhan said don't touch Ruth Angleton."

I grinned because of his smug assurance. "That's all it takes? Nobody wants to be on Darcy Vandiver's shit-list, eh?"

"Absolutely not. And Ruth, it is likely I'll discover who Patient 7 is, but my favor for you is in the future, do not ask his identity. Do we have a deal?"

I nodded. He walked to the exit and with another adios, he was in the elevator and gone. I returned to my office and locked the door, then sat at my desk and pulled open my BMH thread. I would read all of them now, from Heather's first meeting with Jarret to the last.

I care about these women and I care about poor Heather.

The detective's lurid coroner photographs filtered to mind, the pallid faces, the almost-closed eyes, and the sheet pulled to the collarbones on each woman. I couldn't see inside their mouths of course, but I thought about the severed tongues and a Rakum eating them on a full moon. This was wrong. It was inhuman. And I *cared*.

The monsters I treated *didn't care*.

The Rakum inside each transformed vampire didn't care.

But they were human now—if they couldn't be taught to care, they'd eventually all be murderers. I needed a Rakum confederate that cared about these poor women.

David Walker!

I grabbed my purse, turned off my computer and headed downstairs. I'd be in Tuscaloosa in less than an hour. I didn't know if they'd let me in, but I remembered the way to the church.

161

Hell, I'm sure if I tell any of this to their preacher, he'll see me. He has to — followers of Jesus have to care about the innocent women murdered by this monster…

I turned toward the interstate, convincing myself all the way out of town.

An hour later, I sat in a lushly appointed breakfast nook across from a beanpole of a woman who looked upon me with kind brown eyes. The Rakum at the gate had not let me in, but because he remembered Pitch brought me, he gave Walker my message. As a result, the preacher sent me to his home where I waited with his wife, sipping hot chocolate and (so far) talking about anything but vampires, Cows, and psychopaths.

"I don't know if I should mention it, but you are a very striking woman," Polly Anna (no shit, that's her name) said and finished off her cocoa.

"Thanks," I said and hoped I didn't make her feel weird. I didn't know what else to add to such a compliment.

She took a deep breath and rose to walk a few paces to the smooth steel-aproned sink. "David told me about you." She turned her face to see my reaction and I gave her a genuine smile. "He loves all of his brethren so much and prays for them night and day. According to my husband, your man, Kfir, is a bright new star in the church. He's been sharing his testimony and helping so many find peace in the Lord. He takes it on the road, too. Sort of a traveling lay-pastor for the church. You should see them piled into that van, tooling away after Bible study…"

That white van again. It was all I could do to leave it alone. My silence left the air awkward and she returned to her seat.

"You made the right decision to come here tonight. A sin is defined by any rebellious action taken against God or His word. Most sins are action, but some are *lack* of action, *not* helping when you should. David will help you with this investigation."

I had no idea she was so informed but before I could reply, footsteps headed our way. Two men were speaking out of earshot and I recognized Darcy's voice.

Shit! He's going to get in the way!

I put on a passable smile and the Rakum preacher walked in followed by Mr. *I-Won't-Snitch-On-My-Brethren.* David kissed his wife's cheek and she made a polite exit. Then he turned to me and gestured for the next room.

"Let's sit in here," he said and led the way to an amber-lit study with brown bookshelves lining three of the four walls. The fourth wall had been curtained against the night, ceiling to floor, so I imagine during the day, the library received amazing sunlight. "Darcy told me about your earlier conversation, so I think I know where to start."

I sought Darcy's eye and he gave me a wink and a debonair smile. It worked—any frustration I felt about him in the kitchen dissolved. He still had some sort of superpower and he knew it.

I said to David, "After Darcy explained his position, which I appreciate, I thought to myself you guys that follow God must care about these murdered women. That's why I came. Thank you for seeing me like this. I know it was rude to come uninvited."

"Nonsense," David said and watched Darcy slump into an overstuffed recliner. When he turned his face back to me, a sideways grin had hit his mouth—it was the look of someone enamored with the perfection I also saw. David noticed that I noticed and he chuckled. "I didn't know Darcy before. He's a nice-looking guy, eh? Turned Polly Anna inside out first time they met."

"I'm sure," I said and waited to see how he wanted to start.

"To the meat of the issue. As of tonight, I don't know who is killing these women." He turned to see Darcy's face. "Do you know who it is?"

Darcy flit his eyes to mine and back to David before he replied. "I have my theories, but my brothers have not confided this to me."

David stood, crossed to the gigantic pine desk and retrieved a sheet of paper from the shiny surface. "I wrote down all of the clues so far. Darcy ruled out Pitch and Kfir, which helps."

I huffed. "Again with Keifer. There's no way. Why would ya'll even have to say that?"

Both Rakum looked at me without an answer. I waited, certain they must see that my lover could never murder anyone and cut out their tongue. Not now. Not since he's been mortal. They refused to agree so my mind went there. What did they know that I didn't? Keifer had been mortal fifteen months, I met him a little over a year ago. Had he been a murderer *after* 11/13? I had to ask.

"What did Keifer do before I met him? There's a reason you had to rule him out."

"I think he should be the one to tell you, Ruth," David said and looked to Darcy for his take.

Darcy shrugged. "He won't mind." Darcy then said to me as an aside, "David's a great guy but he turned mortal on purpose at Last Assembly.[9] He's a tad out of touch when it comes to his brethren who don't yet know God." He gave Walker a glance, who acquiesced with a nod. "When Kfir woke up human, he did his share of violence

164

upon the mortals around him."

I narrowed my eyes, trying to guess what specific crimes my gentle lover committed and I had no idea how devious I should go. If I asked Darcy, he'd likely be honest, so I steeled my nerve and asked.

"Are you talking straight out murder, or premeditated torture-killing sprees?"

David cleared his throat as if it didn't need to be discussed, but as I thought he might, Darcy replied forthright.

"The latter. We all did. Check the murder stats for early 2019 worldwide, wherever my brethren were assigned. Over time and one by one, we assimilated as best we could."

"All that aside," David said, "now that I know what to look for, all of us at the church will feel out our brethren and find out who it is. He will confess to us and we'll get him help."

"You'll handle it yourselves," I said without emotion and both men nodded.

"The killings will stop. That's your goal, right?"

I looked at both men in turn and sighed. Time to be straight just the way they liked. "Maybe you haven't learned this part yet, but we like to see justice done, which means, we want someone to pay for their crime. An eye for an eye, right?"

Walker picked up right away. "Do you realize that's a biblical principal? And do you know you have used it out of context?"

I shook my head. "I'm not a Bible expert but telling your brother that he was bad and should stop killing isn't justice for the families of the women he's killed. It's not justice to me for losing my friend."

165

David looked to Darcy who rolled his eyes when I caught his gaze. "I won't speak for David; I care about my brethren but that is as far as my altruism reaches."

"What about you?" I asked the preacher. "Aren't you responsible for all God's creatures? Not only the Rakum? Isn't that the way it works?"

Walker gave me a genuine smile that patronized just the same. "Maybe, but I'll need some time to process. There are others more theologically advanced who I turn to for counsel and guidance."

I read the Rabbit book that Pitch recommended, so I knew where he was going. "Those Rakum with Beth Rider, right? Yeah, ask them."

David grinned at the mention of the name. "Yes, exactly, I didn't realize you knew about that." He lifted his phone from the side table and pressed a key. It rang and he put it on speaker.

"Kazak," a male voice said so I assumed it was one of his brothers.

"Mike, got a minute?" David asked and the man on the phone said yes.

I assumed then he was speaking to Michael Stone from the Rabbit-woman's book and I listened with interest. He'd been a vicious Rakum lieutenant for one of their oldest Elders when he met the woman who eventually brought down their entire race. I marveled then and now that the Rakum didn't outright kill her and her entire family because of that alone.

"One of our brothers is murdering women and I'm going to soon know who it is. I can feel it—he's close. Do you think it's enough for us to handle it between us? There is a mortal involved who seeks further justice. What do you think?" David watched my face as he spoke and then

166

listened for a reply. I leaned forward, curious but guessing ahead what the guy would say.

"Handle it in-house," Stone said without pause. *"For a few decades at least, we need to keep our past a secret. The little mortals who know about it will just have to accept that we know what we're doing."*

David smiled and Darcy huffed a laugh at my expense. They made goodbyes and David got to his feet.

"Wait," I said not moving. "Do you honestly think it's okay for your brother to torture and murder people because afterward, he'll apologize to God for it? That is not justice and I don't think God would think so either." I was hot thinking every Rakum that followed Jesus got a free pass. The hypocrisy was too much.

David took a moment to gather his response. "Much like for your people, if we ask God to forgive us, admitting we have sinned, He erases the transgression. But also like with your people, there may be consequences on earth even when your slate is wiped clean." He peeked at Darcy and back again. "Whoever is doing this will be corrected. Here. Among his brothers."

My head hurt and I did not agree at all.

"Would you like to stay here tonight? I wouldn't want you driving home this late," he said, our meeting concluded.

With a sigh of frustration, I also stood and checked the clock wondering where Keifer might be.

Darcy jumped in to help. "Kfir rented an apartment. I alerted him you were here."

"Good," I said grumbling inside that he AGAIN wasn't where I needed him *when* I needed him. "I'll go over there. Darcy, can I follow you?"

The big man agreed without complaint and after

saying goodbye to Polly Anna (still, that name, LOL), I was soon tailing Darcy's dually Ford down the driveway behind the wheel of my beautiful new Maxima. I used the Bluetooth to call Keifer.

"Hey, babe, you heading over?" he asked without a care in the world. I said I was and said no more. Inside, I stored my discontent. I hope I can contain it at his new place. I didn't want to fight, but I don't see how I can let him slide. I mean, he was less than ten miles away and he didn't think it necessary to meet us at David's? How clueless can he be?

My phone rang and the dash read *Det. Paramus* from when I entered his deets at his first call. I hit the Bluetooth.

"We have some new evidence. If I send you a photo, will you see if you can identify anything in it?" the detective asked.

My phone wouldn't receive a text while I was on the line, so I told the man to send it and I'd call him back. I slowed to pull off the road and waved at Darcy when he copied my move. My hand gesture said, *let me use the phone,* and he waited, his truck idling at my bumper, parked on the shoulder.

When I opened the man's text, a photograph appeared of a hand shooting a bird. My mind went to Keifer's pic of Ivan making the gesture at church, but there was no way I could identify a man's hand. What did the cop want? I called him back.

"PD received this from an anonymous caller. It came over as a digital file. Is there anything in it you recognize or might help us identify this man?"

I was speaking through the Maxima, so I looked again at the picture. Caucasian male hand, no freckles, no moles, no jewelry, and the background was dark and featureless, with the camera flash illuminating the subject alone.

"I'm sorry, I don't see how I can tell you anything you

can't see yourself," I said, my eyes to the photo.

"*Okay, how about this,*" he said, sounding irritated. "*The techs read the metadata. This photo was taken with a Canon SLR-D, the newest model. The date stamp puts it around the time the Tuscaloosa woman was found. Does any of that ring a bell?*"

Canon SLR? *Oh, god,* Darcy took a camera like that out of Keifer's desk. *When was that?* I looked at my mental calendar. It was a couple of days after Heather's disappearance. But...

What the fuck, Ruth? There are a zillion cameras like that!

I mumbled to the cop that I couldn't add anything and disconnected.

So Keifer has an SLR.

His friend flipped him off when he took that church pic.

Someone sent the cops a bird from the same brand camera.

None of this meant my boyfriend was a killer, but it was about time he answered some straight questions. I was done putting up with vague misdirection. From all of them, Pitch, Darcy, and David included.

As I got back onto the road behind Darcy to Keifer's apartment, I no longer gave him the Rakum excuse. The closer I got, the more I fumed. Keifer was going to answer some questions and I didn't care how ugly it got. *Not at all.*

The Argument

Keifer was half-naked when he answered my knock. Darcy had followed me up the steps and my lover asked us both inside his new abode. It was a new construction uber-modern apartment complex with posh accoutrements that I barely noticed in my mental fury. I clenched my jaw and stomped past, making an excuse for the restroom. When I came out, Keifer and Darcy were chuckling in the kitchen. It was time to be forthright before I blew my cool.

"We need to speak privately, babe," I said and because of the way his face whipped to mine, I realized he detected an edge to my tone.

"Wait for me in the other room," he said meeting my gaze.

I narrowed my eyes and frowned, but before I had made my exit, Keifer turned back to Darcy to resume their conversation. I left the room, leaned against the wall just on the other side and eavesdropped out of spite.

"What's going on?"

"A cop came to see her and she couldn't reach you."

"…"

They started up with the Rakum Hungarian and I waited for a word I recognized. What did Keifer think I'd do now? Was he purposefully baiting me to fight? In our year together, never had he openly disregarded me; if ever his Rakum behavior came off as gruff or mean, he'd apologize and try again. Lately, since the emergence of Jesus combined with the evil work of Patient 7, his worry over whether or not Ruth was happy seemed to have gone out the window. And Darcy, when did he become such an asshole?

He said it at David's... I have to face the fact that they are still mostly monsters. A few months of therapy after centuries of evil living did not an angel make.

"Fucking tongues..."

I heard those two words in English, but the rest of the phrase was incomprehensible. Then Darcy appeared, walked past me with a wink, and left the apartment. Keifer remained out of sight so I stepped to the kitchen entrance.

He had leaned against the counter facing the door, as if waiting for me to come in. I stared at his face. What was he thinking? He lifted one hand to stroke his sternum, his soft brown chest hair feathering through his fingertips, and he licked his lips. I waited. He waited. As three seconds elapsed, I realized I had no idea who he was anymore.

"I've never eaten a woman's tongue," he said barely audible and holding my eye. "But I've ravaged more than my share in two centuries." I managed a micro-shrug combined with a half-nod before he added, "Are you worried that I might murder you in your sleep?"

My jaw dropped. What had Darcy told him? I stepped full into the room, my eyes on fire.

"At no time have I EVER thought you'd hurt me. Until right NOW!" I had shouted at the end and this time, it was

171

Keifer's eyes that grew small.

"Why now?" he asked in a controlled tone.

"I'm adding things up, *Kfir,*" I said stressing his Rakum name, maybe saying it aloud for the first time. "Since you started up with that church, I can't depend on you. You stopped working this relationship. There's no partnership. I've been fucking CHASING YOU for six weeks and I've had it!"

He tipped his chin. "You've had it? What does that mean in Ruth-talk? Is this a mind game you've devised to put me back in line?"

I didn't care for the evil edge to his voice, and frankly, I'd never heard it before—not in him.

I'd heard it from Rakum I treated.

Wait...

I'd heard it on Heather's recording of Patient 7's initial call-in. My brain flashed white-hot at the thought and I took a step closer.

"Fuck, Keifer! Are you Patient 7? Are you the one calling Heather, admitting all that shit about the women you raped and killed?"

Keifer licked his lips, holding my eye and so far, his face revealed nothing. Not anger, shock, humor, insult—nothing. I rolled over Heather's chat entries, everything Patient 7 confessed to, bragged over. It couldn't be Keifer. I'd know if I was sleeping next to a rapist, a torturer, right? I'd know. I'm a trained psychologist, an expert in human behavior.

He's not human...

My face flushed with the realization and I stepped back. "Patient 7 told Heather he raped, murdered, and mutilated transgendered women across three states..." I watched his eyes and he maintained his fathomless expression. My voice tapered to a whisper to finish with, "Patient 7 fucked them in post-mortem stab wounds..."

"Ask me again," he said, his voice normal as I'd ever heard it. I swallowed and shook my head. "Ask me with respect."

He didn't want to be bossed; hadn't I learned this already? But I had my answer. He didn't have to say anything. I backed another step and he remained against the granite counter edge.

"I'm going home."

"Stay here, with me," he replied following with his eyes as I backed one more time and now stood in the kitchen doorway. "We're getting married, right?" he asked in the same lifeless voice.

I shook my head. "We need a break. You and your brothers can deal with whatever shit is causing you to do this. I'm going home. You call me when you've stopped."

"I've stopped." He finally stood from leaning and took a step my way. "And I didn't kill your friend."

I backed into the living room. "Stop. Just stay there." I pivoted to the foyer and the way the apartment had been laid out, I could reach the front doorknob still holding his eye. I fingered the brass handle and depressed the latch with my thumb. "Tell David Walker. He'll help you."

I opened the door and when I stepped to the threshold, he left the kitchen and joined me in the tiny entryway.

"It's not over between us," he said, a touch of emotion reaching his words if not his eyes. "I'll call you."

"Okay," I said in a whisper and, with an exhale, I left his apartment. I half-expected him to follow, either retrieve me by force or beg me to return, but he did neither. The door closed of its own weight and I took a brisk walk to my car. The night sky was pregnant with storm clouds and the air icy as I reached the Maxima and dropped behind the wheel.

I think Keifer's raping and killing trans women!

But he's not cutting out their tongues? Who is?

He has an accomplice!

That's what he wanted me to ask! He wanted to confess his confederate was among his brethren!

I got my car on the road and focused down on my suspects. Pitch (no way), Darcy (no way), the others at the church? Why not?

I frowned; I had no confidence in dismissing Pitch and Darcy as I had and to fight my growing panic, I switched on the radio and turned the volume to 8. I'd be home in an hour; Billy Idol screamed in my ear and I shoved the Rakum to the back, back, back.

For now.

The Consoler

Once I reached my house and locked myself in, I looked around the space. Keifer and I bought it together. Two names, two social security numbers, two people securing a residence to share and grow in to. Now that my lover was a known murderer, our shared home had lost its color. My head pounded and my heart grieved with loss. I loved him. I still wanted him.

No, Ruth—you want what you thought *he was, what you made him in your mind.*

I faced the dark living room, seeing nothing.

I did that, I saw a Rakum, a vampire, changing into a mortal, doing human things and feeling emotions he never possessed before 11/13; I saw what I wanted to see. Sure, Keifer and the others were transforming, but not at the speed my model showed. I skewed it with personal prejudice—my affection for Keifer slanted my results. I needed to be a scientist again. I needed to return to math and stats and computations.

I pictured Darcy, the way he winked when he passed me to leave Keifer's apartment. What had they been talking about? Had Darcy questioned him about Patient 7? Numbly, I removed my phone from my purse and hit

Darcy's number. He picked up on the third ring.

"What's up?" he asked, his beautiful deep voice as open and friendly as I'd ever heard it. An hour ago, he left me alone with a murderer. *Shit.* That's when I made note of the breathy tenor, as if he was having sex.

"I left Keifer. Is he going to be okay? Will you make sure he gets help?"

Heavy breathing and a chuckle of someone else sounded in my ear and I couldn't tell if his friend was male or female.

"Pitch is taking care of him. Kfir will never be without our support."

I hung up, not wanting to listen to him romancing someone, anyone, when I was so unhappy. I crossed to the stairs and ascended, staring at Pitch's icon. Was Kiefer with him already? And if so, why? Seeking comfort? A commiserating ear? Or maybe Pitch's more physical brand of consolation?

With an angry snort, I pressed the man's icon and entered my bedroom, closing and locking the door once inside. The phone rang seven times and quit with no voicemail option. When I tossed the device to the comforter, it buzzed with an alert. Dreading what I might find—was it another video?—I picked it up as if covered with slime.

Video from Pitch, the banner read. Then, my text message center populated and I read the first few words: *"Your boyfriend came over drunk off his ass. I'll keep him warm."* Sent with a kiss emoji next to a whiskey glass.

I could text back. I could call. I could interrupt whatever shit he was doing and that would show him. But instead, I pressed the blinking video camera icon.

"Whoa, steady there, brother…"

I covered my mouth. Pitch and Keifer stood between a large sofa and a glass-topped coffee table, Keifer decidedly intoxicated and Pitch busily stabilizing him by both shoulders.

"What's going on? You fighting with the doc?" Pitch asked his question while moving into a position to better support Keifer's wobbling weight. *"Did you drink the entire bar?"*

"I'm not junk," Keifer replied and lifted both arms to drape loose about Pitch's neck. My camera angle took in both men in profile and my lover took a moment to balance on both feet and then moved his hands to Pitch's bearded cheeks. It looked like a precursor to kiss, but nothing happened. Keifer held his face and Pitch continued to ask him why he was drunk.

"You want something, brother?" Pitch asked his voice lower than before. *"Want me to call Ruth and iron it out for you?"*

Keifer shook his head. *"She's done with me."*

Pitch slid both hands along the forearms at either side of his head. He was barely an inch taller than Keifer and he caressed Keifer's arms covered as they were in his long-sleeved dress shirt.

"Ah. you need your captain to iron you *out?"* Pitch asked dropping his voice an octave and ducking to snag Keifer's eye.

"Yes," Keifer said with an exaggerated nod. Then without unbuttoning, he yanked his shirt from his slacks and pulled it over his head.

Pitch moved in without delay. Strong hands and stiff fingers ran across, cupping the varying topography—in the precise way I did it, by the way—and all the while, Keifer stood in wobbly balance, hands to Pitch's shoulders now enjoying the attention.

"Okay, brother," Pitch said very softly and I turned up the volume. *"Tell me what happened."*

Without replying, Keifer moved in to kiss Pitch's face and rolled immediately to his mouth. The kiss seemed sloppy and half-hearted and then my lover said against Pitch's cheek, *"She thinks I'm Jeffrey Dahmer."*

"You told her the truth?"

Keifer offered one shake of the head. *"Doesn't matter. It's too hard, fuck this. Come out with me. Let's paint the town red."*

Keifer slurred his last sentence, but I made it out. What did all this mean? He didn't kill the women? Or he did and someone else took their tongues? Maybe I should have stayed and heard more because as I eavesdropped on their conversation, I had more questions than answers.

"I'll tie you up and throw you in the cellar. Would you like that?" Pitch asked and I detected no humor in his voice.

Keifer shook his head with more fervor. *"You and me, we can strike out on our own. I don't want to watch the next fifty years erase the Kfir I was."* Keifer again kissed Pitch's mouth, longer this time, and although his brother didn't push away, I could see Pitch only waited for him to pull back. *"I didn't tell her about Jenny."*

He had said that sentence almost too low for me to hear and their next few words were not in English. What about Jenny? My mind raced, had he hurt her? I considered buzzing her, but I'd have to end the video. As it was streaming in real-time, I didn't know if I could pick it back up. I watched the men talk in their language, listening for a word I understood.

"Then take me to bed," Keifer said in a whisper and Pitch looked to the camera.

What happened next, I can't explain. Pitch covered Keifer's mouth with one hand and hissed, *"Shhh—*

(something in their language)—, *Kfir."* Then, his eyes in mine through the lens, he gave the Rakum expression to be quiet. Then he said as if to me, *"I'll send him to Walker."*

And the feed ended.

I stared at the black phone screen, my brain fuzzing, the past several weeks' events clouding my mind. What just happened? Pitch loved screwing Keifer, and he loved messing with my head. Where did that last moment of empathy come from?

There I go again, making them more than transforming monsters.

Pitch can't learn how to "care" after a few weeks of talk therapy.

JENNY.

A tear sprung to my eye as I pressed her icon. The phone rang until it went to voicemail. I left her message to call me back and I scrolled through my phone for Tiff's cell. Once found, I pressed hers, too. Same result, no answer. My forehead prickled and I looked about the room. It was nearing ten and the storm had arrived. Rain pelted my window in heavy sheets and I considered driving to Jenny's house. Running over a myriad of reasons she and Tiff didn't answer and another set of reasons I didn't need to go out in the rain, I crossed to my bedroom door and opened it to look into the dark hall.

"I didn't tell her about Jenny..."

What had he meant? He said it while collapsing in self-pity, while trying to convince Pitch they should revert to their old ways.

In my hand, my phone dinged and I startled. With gooseflesh covering both arms, I looked at the screen. It came from Pitch's number.

"He's on his way to DW's."

179

I texted back, "He's in no condition to drive!"

"One of our brothers took him. Left 5minutes ago. Chill out. Shit."

"What about Jenny!?!" I typed with extra punctuation.

"I'll look into it. Calm down."

I exhaled, typed a thumb's up, and clicked off the screen.

"Let her be okay," I said to the empty room and backed to close myself inside. My phone rang and I nearly jumped out of my skin. The screen read, unknown number, but because of the circumstances, I answered.

"Dr. Angleton?" an official voice barked and I grunted my reply. "Detective Paramus wants you to know Dr. Jenny Kirkland was reported missing this morning when she didn't return home from a conference."

"What? No. What do you mean, missing? Is Tiff okay?" I collapsed onto my bed and leaned over my knees, afraid to faint but nearly unable to focus my eyes.

"The detective will call you tomorrow. He's out of pocket, but wanted you to know." (click)

"Wait! What?" I scream-shouted and redialed the number. The phone went to an automated response, *"this is an official no-call police line. If you have an emergency, dial…"*

I hit end and dropped my phone on the bed.

What was happening? What happened to my only real friend? WHO happened to my best friend? Had Kiefer done something to her? What did he mean he hadn't told me about Jenny?

I couldn't think straight, exhaustion threatening my very sanity. Heather murdered, that was awful enough. But Jenny?

She's not dead. Shit, Ruth! Geez!

For no good reason, my mind ran over the past few

weeks. Snippets of conversations, newspaper and news reports, things I hadn't officially collated and laid side by side were trying to assemble.

I pictured the work van from the church parking lot, the night Pitch took me there. A witness said the killer in Tuscaloosa spoke to a woman from a white van. Polly Anna said Keifer and his brothers take the van out to do God's work. I shivered. Were they taking the van out to kill people? Was it the same van? I couldn't know and was guessing. But the coincidence…

And the specific brand of camera, and Ivan's hand shooting a bird.

Keifer wouldn't answer straight when I asked him if he was Patient 7. *Why didn't I wait for his reply?*

Detective Paramus thought it important for me to know about Jenny's disappearance. About the evidence he collected on Heather—

Pink silica.

The labeled plastic bag the cop showed me returned to mind. I tracked that stuff myself whenever I left my office. That meant Keifer could have walked through my transfer here at home and then tracked it to Heathers'.

Wait. It's at my home.

Anybody—any Rakum—could have tracked it if they came here as Keifer's guest.

My mind was crashing and I sat on my bedcovers. I relaxed the grip on my phone to drop it to the mattress when it slipped to the rug. Barely aware of my movements with my brain zooming over all the clues, I dropped to my knees fishing blindly for the cell. I missed twice and knocked it under the bed with my frantic movements.

"Shit shit shit!" I hissed and dropped lower to look beneath the bed. My hand grasped the phone as my eye was drawn to a tiny light far across the king-size space. What was that? On my hands and knees, I crawled the circumference of the bed and looked for the item. It was some sort of router.

Keifer's hidden cameras?

With a gasp I jumped to my feet and resumed the half-hearted search from the other night. Recalling from various movies and TV shows that some of the cameras are wireless and very small, I began turning over things I skipped before. In less than five minutes, I reached a harmless-looking trophy, sitting center, on the top-most shelf of our bookcase. It was a knickknack I'd purchased with him on our first date, a jubilant male character in a business suit pumping his fists in victory. The brass nameplate read, "Best Man for the Job." At the time, it was a joke about how Keifer was the most wonderful man I had ever dated.

I pulled it down and turned it over and around.

A camera, the lens smaller than an English pea, its wire formed inside the trophy about two inches.

Every hair on my head stood on end. What had he done? And why? And who did he send videos to? Not Pitch; I knew this to my innermost parts. But any of the others? Darcy? Ivan? Jarret? The entire Rakum website?

I was close to passing out. Every millisecond of abuse that I endured by my father and my stepfather rushed back with power. Even Aaron, although he only videotaped us once during an overnight church camp, filled my thoughts as if he stood in the room with me. I was suddenly seven, I was eleven, I was twelve... Then I was nineteen, gang-banged by El-A in the apartment he put me in.

I had to get out.

I needed a friend.

JENNY!

But she was missing.

Panicked, I put my feet to the floor. My knees were shaky but I was not giving up. I would go to the only person who had me on his mind 24/7. I jogged down the stairs, grabbed my purse, and was out the door.

I can't tell you anything about the next one hundred miles. It had been sprinkling when I ran to my car in Bessemer, Alabama, but only when I shoved the gearshift to Park in Columbus, Mississippi, did I return to cognizance.

Sheeting rain assaulted my exposed skin as I ran from my car to Pitch's porch. At least, I hoped this was the correct front door. I'd followed the GPS and didn't use a brain cell for anything but worry, anger, confusion and concern. I didn't look for a bell but hammered the wood with a closed fist. Was he even home?

"Pitch! Let me in!" I yelled at the top of my voice, certain the simultaneous thunder drowned out my plea. "Pitch!" I screamed again and turned to look at my car pelted by what now appeared to be pebble-sized hail.

I had reached the place just in time, for the wind whipped through the covered porch erasing every last bit of warmth from my bones. I'd been soaked through on my passage from the car and as it began to dawn on me that Pitch might not be home, a sob escaped and I turned a full circle. Water sloshed in my shoes and I wondered what to do next.

All that time, all that time… I thought I had found my knight in shining armor. I thought he was the one man in the world that wouldn't hurt me. All that time, he was… what? Exorcising his demons with women he met at bars? On the street corner? What?

With all my power, I focused on my tears, willing them

to cease. Why should I fall apart? Was this injury any worse than what I had survived already? I looked at my car roof, the hail bounced with more weight, a true thunderstorm had arrived. I would hear tornado sirens soon and the rain had grown thick enough to reduce visibility to less than twenty feet.

Then, with the pounding of water on the earth and structures all around me, I heard a man's voice and then gentle hands grasping my shoulders.

"Ruth! Get in here! Fuck! You're melting!"

The tender grip swiveled me to look into his face.

Pitch.

When our eyes met, my sobs returned and his eyebrows arched with mortal concern.

"You're okay, you're okay, come here," he said with a sad smile. He folded me into his chest and bodily walked me across the threshold into the foyer. "Shit, look at you. What are you doing?" He stopped us in the center of the marble entryway and sought my eye, leaning out of our embrace without removing an ounce of his support.

"Keifer," is all I said and fell into his chest once more. Pitch chuckled low, a nice sound, a caring sound, and stroked the top of my head with one hand, the other arm firmly behind my back.

"Okay, Kfir," he said and leaned out again. "Take this off." Pitch used both hands at my lapels to drop my Northface jacket to the floor. It landed with a wet flop and he gestured for the buttons of my silk blouse. "Take these clothes off and leave them in the floor."

He spun away and I stood in place, balancing as if intoxicated. But I was only drunk with despair, my arms out from my body and for the moment, only wanting Pitch to return and tell me everything was going to be okay.

He did return, carrying an enormous man sized fuzzy brown robe. When my eyes lifted to his, he held the garment in one hand and pointed to my top button.

"Go on. Get those off and put this on."

I touched my shirt between my breasts, the material lay against my skin running water. I understood he wanted me to remove my wet clothing, but I was paralyzed with shock. Three hours of wondering what would happen if Keifer was the killer, if he'd taped us in bed and shared it online, and wondering if Pitch would even be able to help me. I made a whimpering noise and Pitch lowered his chin, the gentle smile returning, and he came close.

"Lift your arms like this," he said and lifted his half-way with the robe clasped in his right hand.

I did so and he flipped it over his shoulder and used his fingers to unbutton my shirt. I only watched, my nose clogged with crying snot, and he caused it to slide off, down my arms to splash onto the stone floor. I shivered and brought my arms to cross before me and Pitch swirled the robe through the air and across my shoulders. Once it rest there, he slipped his forearms underneath on either side of my torso and nimble fingers unhooked my brassiere. He left it to me to drop it free and I did, and clutched the lush terrycloth tight in front. Then his hands were at my bellybutton and I looked down, the parting of the robe revealing his attentions undoing my leather belt and then the top button of my slacks.

"Fucking masher," I whisper-laughed despite everything and just hearing my voice release something other than anguish made me feel better. Pitch had the zipper down and I stepped out of my loafers and then my sopping wet slacks. He backed away assuming I'd slide off my panties while hidden inside the robe. Once that was done, he waited for me to kick off my socks and he gave me a new grin.

"Now get your silly ass before the fire." His strong hand guided me by the upper arm to the next huge space and right against a roaring wood-burning fire. "Hold on," he said and left me long enough to drag an old-style cane rocking chair to the hearth. He draped the cold wood with a nearby quilt and motioned for me to sit. When I did, he disappeared only to return with an enormous microfleece thick blanket that he flipped out and over my entire form.

"Okay, Doc," he said with a tiny chortle and he dropped to the rug before me, forced my knees apart with a comic noise, and scooted into the space to use both palms, rubbing up and down against my upper arms, looking right into my face from below.

"Pitch," I said and stopped, afraid the tears would restart. I could barely breathe from the earlier snot buildup and I finally brought one hand to my nose. "I need a tissue…"

"Okay, baby," he said sounding kind and worried. "I'll bring you a box. Sit here until you're warmed up a little and I'll bring a towel for your hair."

I nodded and after three more rough rubs, he rolled away and jogged out of the room. I watched him disappear and the strangest emotion pierced my heart, a panic, really, of, *What if he never comes back!* But he did, a box of Kleenex in one hand and a deep green bath towel in the other.

"Thank you," I mewled when he handed over the tissues. He got directly behind me and began swabbing my hair in the towel, expertly wrapping it up, massaging to sponge up the water.

"This is a fucking mess," he said in a laugh and patted it down with his hands when he'd done all he could. "You'll

186

need to get in the shower to straighten this shit out."

I laughed a small sound and blew my nose until my ears reopened. Pitch dragged a matching rocking chair close and sat, leaning forward, his knee inches from mine. He waited for me to look up and I did after I tossed my used tissues into the flame.

"You should wear waterproof mascara, Doc. You look like a horror movie victim."

His eyes searched my face, my lips and eyes and back again, and I discerned huge affection in his expression. It wasn't unfamiliar, I think he always liked me on some level, but tonight, both of us had let some measure of barrier down.

I was still cold. He had mentioned a shower. I thought of standing under hot jets of water and suddenly felt it was the only way I'd warm up.

"Can I get a shower?" I asked as if requesting something more valuable than gold.

Pitch got to his feet. "Right this way, Princess," he said. "My shampoo doesn't smell like honeysuckle, but it makes my hair gorgeous."

I gave him a weary smile, but I meant it. Pitch had become my hero. Right there, right then, offering me his toiletries, allowing me access to his private sanctum. He led me across a wide sitting room to a set of double floor-to-ceiling doors which he swished open with one hand, still guiding me with his other.

We crossed his bedroom and I noted his unmade bed with the same maroon duvet I'd seen in the videos made in this space.

The videos.

My eyes went to a corner that would have held a camera to view the room. Pitch followed my gaze and

187

made a small noise. He gestured with one finger to a cardboard box in the corner filled to the brim with electronics, cords, and what looked like video equipment.

"My cameras are down. All of them," he said low.

I read his eyes and gave a small nod.

We continued then, heading to the bathroom, the one he and Darcy had made love in not so long ago. The pain in my heart expanded then as I remembered my lover had broken me with his treachery, abandoned our vow, and his captain of a hundred years now led me more tenderly than I ever thought possible.

We were now in the bright white space with the gigantic glass-doored shower stall directly in front of me. Pitch pressed a wall panel and the shower started. He turned to face me and after an amused last look at my overall dishevelment, he pointed to a cabinet.

"Towels, soap, wash cloths, toothbrush, whatever I have, just go for it. I think Darcy left some of his shit in there and he is huge on smelling nice." He laughed at his words and looked ready to leave me to it. Before he stepped back, my hand shot out of its own accord and I grasped his elbow.

"Stay with me," I said very small, holding his eye. If he said no, I'd... I'd...

"Doc," he said and stepped close again. "Poor thing, look at you," he said even softer, his eyes searching mine and filled with concern. He brought both hands first to my shoulders and then to my cheeks. "You look like a drowned rat." He grinned and pulled my forehead to his mouth. "I have a thing for rats, you know," he said and kissed my cheek, first one and then the other. "You're going to let me fix you up?" he asked and he touched his lips to mine, but only with the weight of a feather before

188

pulling back to look into my face.

I nodded. "Please," I said in a whisper. "Please fix me up."

"Okay," he said matching my volume and he dropped the contact to unbutton and remove his shirt. Holding my eye, he undid his jeans and kicked them and his shorts away. I still clutched the borrowed robe about my body and he waggled his brow. "Don't get Pitch's robe wet, Princess."

I gave him another weary grin and with a quick inhale, I released my grip on both lapels. The brown robe fell away and Pitch held my eye. He returned his palms to my shoulders and slid them to gently encompass my throat. Only then did he drop his gaze, his eyes caressing my skin, from my throat, to my sternum, and then both breasts with equal respect, and my soft middle and down my thighs.

"Goddammit, Ruth, you must be the most beautiful woman in the world," he said his voice full of sincere awe.

I knew I wasn't, I couldn't be, but something about my body or my essence or my *being* made this gorgeous man think I was more than little abuse survivor Ruth Angleton.

"Come here," he said and draping one arm around my back he led me into the shower. Three heads pelted us with liquid warmth and Pitch pulled me close in the center of them, wrapping me up in his arms and holding me against his body. "Stand here and tell me when you get warm, okay?"

I only nodded into his chest and he lowered his chin to rest a cheek to the top of my head. We stood under the hot water a long time and I eventually got warm. Before my skin had completely pruned, Pitch reached behind him for a washcloth and used it to gently remove the mascara from beneath my eyes. And after that, with a bottle of Axe shower gel on the cloth, he washed my entire body, extreme care and gentleness on every part of me. The last thing he did once he'd made certain every bit of soap washed away was dollop his Old Spice shampoo into one palm to massage into my waist-length hair. I let him do it all, standing there, allowing him to worship me, to care for me, as if I truly was a princess to a Rakum prince. He'd done this before, it was obvious, in another life, he had cleansed and cared for a female in this way, probably for his master, but none of that mattered. For an hour, the Rakum that came to my office to berate, injure, and verbally abuse me was erasing it all. Every stroke of his gentle palms erased the evil words and deeds he'd committed against me over the past two months.

When my hair was rinsed, he made a noise in his chest. I met his eye and he grinned.

"You're done," he said and when I smiled, he leaned in and pressed his lips to mine. There were no tongues, but we had melted together in that kiss. He held me there, mouth to mouth, for a long moment, and then pulled away.

With a wave of his hand near the wall panel, the water trickled off and he touched the glass door. I watched him grab a towel from the closest rack, for the first time allowing my eyes to look him over. He was as beautiful to me as I was to him, and once I received the bath sheet, he toweled off, too, watching my movements. Then he left the bath nude only to return five seconds later wearing boxer briefs. In his hand, he held some clothing and he set it on the sink counter.

"I have a hair dryer," he said pointing to the same cabinet as earlier. "Dry your hair and come find me when you're done. Good?"

I offered a tiny nod. He swabbed his hair with the same towel with which he'd dried his body. He then tossed it to the floor to leave the bathroom. I watched him go; he closed the door three-quarters and was gone.

I'm going to fuck him.

I hadn't planned to go there in my mind but as I dug out the hairdryer and rustled up a brush, I did. I decided it was going to be wonderful.

20

The Plantation

The morning arrived and I hadn't had sex with Pitch. Amazing, I agree.

Last night after I donned what he left me—a pair of boxer briefs and a clean white undershirt—I stepped into the bedroom. He wasn't there. With a curious *humph,* I toddled to the doors and peeked into the quiet hallway. Way, far, at the other end of the huge floorplan, I saw a light filtering from a room off the hall and I padded toward it barefoot, lush carpeting making every step a pleasure. I reached the doorway and Pitch was there folding clothing from a dryer. He looked up and gave me a wink. He gathered the garments into a neat stack and when I reached for them, he shook his head.

"Nah-ah," he said and swirled one finger to tell me to turn around and head back the way I came. With an amused grin, I did and he followed, all the way back to his bedroom. "We might lose power, so there's a flashlight on your side of the bed."

My side of the bed? I looked and saw the nightstand, sitting on it a miniature flashlight and a bottle of Evian. I realized how odd it was that I didn't feel anything negative about him assuming I'd sleep there, and with him, but I still felt cleansed of everything he put me through. He had been redeemed. Now, he was able to begin abusing me again, and I'd watch out for it. But what if…

"Now get under the covers," he said and didn't move until I eyed him a minute and did as he said. Once I had arranged the thick maroon duvet, crisp sheets, and a perfectly sized feather pillow, he clicked off the corner lamp and crawled in on his side.

I recalled this scene, Pitch over there and Darcy where I now lay. How many lovers had Pitch had in this bed? It didn't matter and I wouldn't ask, but the question came to me nonetheless. I looked at him as he arranged his end and when it was just right, he gave me the exact same finger gesture, a swirl in the air.

I gave him a new sideways grin. "You're bossy as shit."

He swirled the finger once more and I rolled onto my side, facing the bathroom door. Pitch reached for my waist, right at my belly button and pulled me into his body, bending his knees into the backs of mine, until his chin rested at my neck from behind.

"Now, go to sleep, Doc."

I lay my arm atop his, no tattoos there like Keifer had. Pitch's tattoos were across his chest, two dragons breathing fire and facing one another. Tonight was the first time I could see them well enough to discern the image. But Pitch's arm was strong, protecting, maybe shielding me from danger, from heartache, from Keifer.

I stroked his arm once. "Thanks," I said low.

"Go the fuck to sleep," he said at the same volume.

Despite the hell of the day—and it had seemed like hell—I smiled and closed my eyes. Sleep came fast and I welcomed it.

Now it's day and sunlight streamed through open curtains in the ceiling-high windows (I'm sure they were closed last night). I was alone in Pitch's bed. Still on my back, I propped up on my elbows and looked about. An elegant wall clock graced the far wall and it read 10:25. That's when I noticed the aroma of breakfast—bacon, eggs, toast, coffee, the works—and my stomach grumbled.

Is he cooking for me? It didn't seem possible, but then, last night also didn't seem within the realm of Pitch's abilities. I rolled off the bed and stretched. As I lowered my arms, I noted my clothes, clean, dry and folded sitting on the bedside stool. With a satisfied exhale I put them on, folding my borrowed clothes to leave in the same way. I visited the bathroom, checked my hair and my phone for messages (none, damn that Keifer), and now, I needed to find my host.

Following my nose, I found the entrance to a large industrial style kitchen with three ranges and two large stainless-steel refrigerators. A stout woman in black slacks, shirt, and apron, turned her face to me and pointed down the way I had been headed.

"You'll find Mr. Ashley in the study, ma'am," she said in a decided Mississippi drawl.

I nodded and continued on. Mr. Ashley? Because of his plantation-style estate, the first thing that came to mind was Ashley Wilkes from *Gone with the Wind*. I reached the study and found my host leaning on a desktop, studying blueprints visible from where I stood. He wore dark indigo blue jeans and a pastel yellow sweater; holy shit, he was better looking than ever in this brand-new day.

He met my gaze, his eyes more green than hazel in this light. He smiled. "It's the princess!" Pitch waved me in.

"You look ready for the next battle."

"I am thanks to you," I said and put extra emphasis on the last word. Did he know how huge his help had been last night? Could he know how close I had come to the end of my frayed rope?

He waved one hand. "We'll eat some breakfast and then go find Kfir. Settle this shit once and for all."

I nodded, but there was more to my appreciation, more to say on his entire late-night rescue. I parted my lips and he held up one hand.

"Enough, hush now about last night." Pitch came from behind the desk and stepped into my space. As familiar as a lover, he lifted his left hand to cup my throat and leaned in to kiss my forehead. "I'm not into discussing deep shit about why, what, when, where, and how. Just be happy and let's eat."

I agreed and when he leaned away, his fingers gentle on my neck, I met his eye. "One thing—you didn't come after me. I just..." I ran out of words and he raised his brow.

"I fell out of character, eh? Walker said I'd rape you; I know. I'm aware of his bias against yours truly. But never fear; you and I will have our fuck session in our own time." He dropped his hand and passed me for the doorway. "For now, let's eat. Rescuing sexy ladies and not ravaging them has left me famished."

I smiled but he had gone. In the kitchen, he sat me at a four-person round dinette and made sure I had a bit of everything. Besides the cook, a young man dressed in the same attire, came close and filled a coffee mug and handed me a glass of water. His nametag read, Oliver, and the company label was Deep South Silver Spoon Catering.

I bit into my toast and Pitch dug into his scrambled eggs, and for that moment, my myriad worries disappeared and I couldn't imagine anywhere in the world I would rather be.

The Search

I allowed Pitch to drive me back to Alabama. I mean, how could I ever see him the same way after that tender scene at his place? I didn't know when or if he'd drop the other shoe, but I decided his sins were forgiven and I'd await new ones to hate him for.

Currently, we were tooling east, only an hour out of Columbus, and so far, the conversation had been light and meaningless. With a glance in the side mirror, I made out my Maxima. Because he could, Pitch hired a man to drive my car home. They had a business for such a thing (yay, capitalism!) and I appreciated that they seemed to enjoy the speed limit.

The brilliant Mississippi sun erased any evidence of last night's hailstorm.

"I checked the website," he said, eyes on the road. "Kfir posted no open videos from his account." He peeked my way and resumed driving. "He can send things privately to brothers that I wouldn't know about, but when I ask him, he will tell me the truth."

My chest tightened at the thought of the upcoming

confrontation, but Pitch's presence gave me courage. Then, he handed me his iPhone, his eyes on the road.

"Text Kfir. Say, *mare-theh-vaggy.*"

With a friendly huff, I instead hit the microphone and pushed it to Pitch's face. He said the foreign phrase into the phone which then spelled it out.

"That's what? Hungarian?" I figured their phones could not possibly speak their language.

"Yeah, it means 'where are you'."

Pitch glanced at me and I wondered what he wanted to say. For whatever reason, for the first time, he did not speak his mind. I waited, watching his profile and not willing to confront him on bottling up. The longer he didn't speak, the more my mind wondered what he wouldn't say. In the end, I broke the silence.

"You've never held your tongue before. Say it," I said in what sounded like a normal tone.

Pitch sucked his teeth once before beginning with an exhale. "I told you I felt different about you the past few weeks. Last night, I wanted to protect you..."

He laughed the last word and I remained quiet, watching him from the side. He turned to shoot me a smile; the one that melts a woman's last resolve. For a tiny moment, I had never seen a more beautiful man—it's just, I can't explain it.

"Before this human change in your pal, I maintained my distance on purpose." He shot me a new look, this one apologetic. "In general, I was honest in our sessions. What I haven't been honest about is what you don't know about *us*. About me, Kfir, and Ivan."

My ears perked. What the hell had Keifer done that was so awful? I didn't ask as Pitch appeared ready to speak.

"Tell me how you met Kfir," he said giving me the

impression my answer would prompt his next share.

"Okay. I had dropped off some bags of clothing for the Salvation Army in Hoover and drove past a coffee shop with a long line of people out the front door. I pulled in to grab a cup and sit in the sun and while in line, I was bumped by a man throwing away his trash. It was Keifer."

"You knew on sight that he was a Rakum?"

"I had no doubt."

"This was in January of 2019?" he asked and I nodded. "There's a lot you're unaware of because you haven't had a need to know..." He rolled in his bottom lip as if thinking of the right words.

"I don't understand."

"Kfir told you he used to bunk with me, right? In the Old Days?"

I nodded.

"We purposefully keep our details vague when dealing with mortals. Now that we're human, and..." He tossed me a new wink, "...now that I like you..." He comically faked a shiver and continued. "...there are a few things I could tell you that may shed light on your Patient 7 quest."

"Is it Keifer? It is, isn't it?" I whispered.

Pitch shrugged. "I don't know. None of the brethren confess to me. They confess to *Darcy,*" he said and then mimed oral sex with a closed fist bumping at his mouth.

I said in a small voice, "When I played the recording of Patient 7's initial call-in, it sounded like Keifer."

"Sounded like him? Or was him?"

"I can play it for you," I said and used the cord to connect my phone to his audio. In another few seconds I had pulled up the chatroom. He nodded. I hit play and the man's voice sounded from the expensive Bose speaker system. My eyes remained on his profile; his eye narrowed and he exhaled when it ended.

"Do you have any other recordings of this guy?" he asked and I said no.

"Heather didn't record the sessions. I don't either."

"Good girl," he said and shot me a new look. "The voice—it's a brother, but it sounds like someone pretending to be Kfir, or who spent a lot of time with him. Which brings us back to topic—"

"What I don't know..."

Pitch dove in. "I've known Kfir more than a century and our duties as Rakum soldiers required we cohabitate. But I think for the current purpose, I'll start at 11/13."

When he paused for a response, I only nodded.

"When we lost our birthright, I sought him out. Our website was just starting up and I wanted my favorite soldiers under me." He gave a devil's chuckle and I allowed it. "I found Kfir, who had been with Ivan, close and tight, since Last Assembly."

"Last Assembly," I repeated. In the *Rabbit* book,[10] she described how the Rakum were left leaderless and exposed. They were all still vampires but hid from each other due to the confusion of that trauma. I murmured for him to continue.

"We huddled together in my Buffalo apartment, transforming and angry as hell."

"This fits what I know, only Keifer left out the details and he never mentioned Ivan." I thought back to the ballet. Keifer had pretended he hadn't seen the guy in ages. My mind ran over the English parts of their conversation. Ivan mentioned the tongues...

Pitch continued. "When Ivan joined the household, he brought his specific mental baggage and I didn't care. Kfir had shit in his head, too. Hell, all I wanted to do was squeeze the life out of every mortal I met."

I nodded, recalling a conversation about their anger when Kiefer and I were getting acquainted. Although, I never put two and two together, that my newly-human lover had raped or murdered anyone. I distanced myself—which was more evidence that I skewed my data for some awesome sex with a former blood drinker.

"And we didn't talk much. Rakum don't banter like mortals," he said and huffed, adding as if to himself, "of course, we can't shut up now that we're human." He shook his head. "The point I'm trying to make… Fuck! I'm boring as shit…"

"No, go on. Please, I need this," I said.

"In bed, Kfir and Ivan were there for my benefit. They didn't discuss their kills or assaults or victories over your kind. This means, I don't know what they were up to when their captain wasn't around. What we did together, I can tell you about. But only if you think it will give you peace. None of my experiences are for any mortals other than yourself. Do you understand?"

"I know, I get it. Darcy explained it, that he would never turn a brother in no matter what he did. Darcy thinks David Walker and his guys will counsel the one who did the killings and that will be enough."

"I feel the same way." Pitch checked his mirrors and continued. "11/13 around midnight, I was fucking one of my Cows. Whatever mystical shit the Elders did that night to steal my birthright left me breathless and panicked. I'd never been panicked before and I choked the woman to death to hush her screaming."

He shot me a glance I understood; she had lost her Cowness at the same instant and was likely desperate to leave.

"Yes," he said reading my eyes. "It took me three weeks to shed my light sensitivity and I didn't handle it well, attacking randomly. It's amazing I wasn't found out by the mortal authorities because I wasn't careful. I finally found Kfir and Ivan and they arrived with blood on their hands."

"I've given this a lot of thought, of what it would be like to be king of the world one night and wake up basically, a toad."

Pitch huffed once. "Did Kfir tell you that I was the one that talked him into getting help with his issues?"

He glanced at me and I widened my eyes. I hadn't heard that and it seemed important, since it was Keifer who convinced Pitch to get help later.

"At the time, I hadn't accepted any of it. Kfir had. He sought balance and wanted to figure out how to be a human. I'm the one that found Big Viv."

"Big Viv?" I repeated, picturing a six-foot female truck driver.

"Yes, Big Viv. Most of my brethren wanted to assimilate. We're extremely intelligent; each of us understood that if we didn't figure it out, we'd end up shot by police or incarcerated."

I nodded. "Keifer said some of your brothers preferred prison. That they were happy to inflict misery on others for the rest of their days and if they were arrested, they enjoyed making prison life hell for all."

Pitch agreed. "That was almost me, which is why Kfir suggested I get help." He hooked a thumb in my direction before returning that hand to the wheel. "Big Viv was the Career Counselor for the women's penitentiary in Buffalo. Before Last Assembly, she'd been a Cow to a compatible brother named Avi. Over the course of years, she used her counseling skills to treat anger issues among the inmates and had the idea to help the Rakum if she could find them. She posted ads in large newspapers as well as on the Cow website for free group counseling for Rakum. That keyword caught my brethren's attention and when I saw it, I gave the info to Kfir. Suggested he call her and see if she might help him."

"That was nice," I said as a reflex but Pitch shook his head.

"No, Princess, I was watching out for my self-interests. Kfir was always my favorite companion. His constant bitching would have driven me insane; I didn't want to have to choke him in his sleep." Pitch finished with a single chuckle, but I think he was serious.

"Big Viv helped him?"

"Big Viv—she gave herself that name—invited us to participate in group therapy. I didn't go. Kfir and Ivan did, where they met a third brother named Jarret."

"Patient 6," I said under my breath. "Why would Jarret go to Big Viv in New York and a few months later, become a patient to Heather in Alabama?"

"I never cared before, but if we find him at the church tonight, I'm going to ask him."

"Are you sure we should?" I asked and imagined facing down a dozen Rakum as the only female in the building.

In lieu of an answer, Pitch hit the Bluetooth in the dash and the phone rang through the car's speaker system.

"Kazak," a man's voice said and I didn't recognize it right off. "He's here."

"Kazak," Pitch replied and then spoke in their language. The banter lobbed back and forth and when he pressed end, he sighed.

"What is it? Who was that?" I asked.

"That was Jarret. He's with Ivan and Kfir alone. No meetings tonight. When we get there, we'll have privacy. We can ask Kfir what he knows about the murders."

"He killed someone since I met him, hasn't he?" I asked and didn't truly want to know.

Pitch peeked my way and refocused on the road. "I was telling you the Big Viv story for a reason."

"Okay, I'm sorry. Go ahead."

"Kfir, Ivan and Jarret attended her classes four nights a week for three weeks. She fancied them, all three, and this I heard from Ivan one night some weeks later. After each session, she'd turn from counselor to courtesan and take them to bed."

"Oh, geez," I said embarrassed for her and in my mind, she was still driving an eighteen-wheeler.

"We don't turn down sex—even mortal." He didn't look over, but I think he smirked, likely thinking of last night when we did nothing sexual the entire night.

"Okay... so?"

"Big Viv held these sessions at her house to keep it off the books. The night she decided they had graduated, they had an orgy, hard drugs were involved." This time, he peeked over, and I held my face static. "I don't have the details, but Ivan later told me that the woman died."

"What? How?" I asked as if waking up to the seriousness of the issue.

"We can ask them tonight. At the time, I didn't care."

With a slow nod, I pondered all he shared. "That was January last year," I said repeating the dates and he nodded. "I met him at the coffee shop like... *mere days* after he did this to this woman..." I shook my head in slow motion. How did I not see anything suspicious? Am I not as fantastic a therapist as I thought? I needed to tuck that nugget away and ponder it later. I veered back on course. "Maybe Ivan is Patient 7."

Pitch made no reply. Up ahead, I saw a sign for our exit and I concentrated on being calm.

"Let me ask you something," I said in a bit of clarity. "Keifer assured me that the Rakum weren't cannibals, ya'll enjoyed blood and violence, but you didn't eat flesh, right?"

Pitch shrugged more or less.

"When he first heard that the victim's tongues had been severed, I asked if his brother was eating them. Keifer got the weirdest look on his face, like wistful, and he said, 'might be'."

"He was saying yes," Pitch stated with authority.

I blinked and rolled on. "We went to the ballet and ran into Ivan. When they talked about the murders, Ivan looked at me and said, 'the tongue talks.'" I shook my head. "I didn't like him."

Pitch hadn't made a sound or reaction. I added more.

"What about this. Keifer and Ivan acted like they hadn't seen each other in years. Why would he do that? Disguise the fact that he had seen Ivan more recently? In hindsight, it looks as if they're colluding."

Still Pitch remained silent and I watched his profile.

"Keifer once told me that he and Ivan liked mortals, enjoyed our quote, soft places, and you hated us."

Pitch nodded. "I haven't lied about that. I like you now, but I spent my life trying to make the humans cry. It was a great game."

Pitch's phone chimed with a text and he gestured for me to read it for him. It was in English and I read it. *"They left."*

205

"Shit," Pitch hissed and pressed the Bluetooth. "You stay the fuck right there, jerkoff," he said when a man answered his call. Pitch pressed end and turned onto the church's long drive.

I took a deep breath and worked to remain calm.

The Answers

In another five minutes, we had entered the huge main room, empty as reported. I remained directly behind Pitch as he strode across the space. He reached the room's only occupant and the guy took a step back.

"Hell, Pitch, chill the fuck out. I didn't see them leave. I had to take a shit."

"Ivan and Kfir disappeared while you took a shit?" Pitch asked patronizing.

Jarret leveled his gaze and had not yet met my eye. "You know those two. They're probably in the Tahoe fucking." When Pitch only growled, he shrugged. "What do you want from me? I don't know."

Pitch moved in, bullying the shorter man who again shrank back. Whatever their history, it would appear then and now, Pitch was the man's superior. "What do you know about these murdered women? The dead psychoanalyst?"

"Nothing," Jarret replied in an exasperated whine and Pitch took him by the bicep.

"I'm done with your shit. Tell me what you know

about these killings. About the dead psychotherapist."

Jarret's eyes flit to me for the first time and he said something incomprehensible to Pitch.

"Yes, and in English. You were Dr. Flank's patient. Who came in after you?" Pitch sounded truly fed up and it seemed Jarret discerned the same thing.

Jarret licked his lips. "I can't believe you don't know."

Pitch grabbed his lapel with such speed that I startled and hopped backward.

"It's us, okay, shit! Me, Ivan and K. We called her. Took turns. It was fun. Let me go and I'll explain, fuck!" Pitch opened his hand. "Dr. Flank graduated me out to get rid of me. I wasn't done. Not by a mile."

"Go on," Pitch said low.

"Fuckin' dikes, cock-sucking mixed-up queers! They'd say yes to Kfir and turn their asshole noses up at me and Ivan. So, we made up a new game. That's all…"

I started to ask a question and stopped, realizing I wasn't in my office and my doctor hat was not welcome. But Pitch turned his face to mine, a respect there I had missed before.

"Go ahead, Ruth."

I swallowed. "How did this start? There's an origin…" (I gulped). "The three of you… Why the tongues?" My questions faded out. I wanted psychiatric reasons for something vampires did.

Hello? Ruth?

But Jarret answered as if he enjoyed hearing his own voice.

"Big Viv." He looked at us both. "The night she died…" He cut his eyes to me. "Kfir had her by the throat, fucking her brains out."

I didn't give him the satisfaction of an expression, so

he returned his attention to Pitch.

"She always liked it rough, but she had this coke and we were wasted. Ivan was done, I finished, and as Kfir closed the deal, the woman died. No fanfare, no struggling, just her eyes dilated and she was gone. Ivan went bananas, hooting and tripping. Me and Kfir sat back and watched him fuck her again and then he tried to find more places to poke and poke and poke and we just watched and laughed."

I was horrified at the picture he created but somehow held my face still. Thankfully, he was speaking to Pitch and not me anymore.

"Somewhere in that melee, we fell asleep. When we awoke, we were sober. Big Viv was dead. We moved her body to the bathtub and that's when I noticed she had bled from the mouth. When I looked closer, she was missing her tongue." He looked at me to add, "I collected tongues for my master in the Old Days, it was his hobby. I think I must have cut hers out while we were tripping."

"Did you eat it?" I whispered.

"I don't remember, but it was nowhere to be found." He looked back to Pitch. "I told all of this to David. He's taking care of it. He's going to help me."

"Did you kill Heather?" I asked in a soft voice.

"No. But I think Ivan did." He pointed a knuckle my way. "All of this is Kfir's fault. He never should have treated Ivan the way he did."

"What did Kfir do?" I whispered as Pitch had invited me to speak freely.

Jarret looked at Pitch as if I was clueless. "Doesn't she know about Ivan and Kfir?"

"They lived together. And?" I said.

Pitch sighed and considered Jarret before gazing off

into the dark church space. "It's like this, Ruth. Mortals cling, Rakum don't." He sucked his teeth choosing his words. "After 11/13, Ivan clung to Kfir but the mortal attraction was one-way. When I found them, Kfir jumped into my bed as if Ivan didn't exist. I'm their superior, so the shit never complained to my face, but over time, I saw his jealousy when Kfir and I were together."

"Ivan was in love with Keifer?"

"That's as good a way to say it as anything."

I shook my head, for now, only pretending to understand. "Ivan's jealousy fueled these murders?"

Pitch looked at Jarret. "Tell us about the first woman who died after Viv."

Jarret shrugged. "After Viv, Kfir and Ivan stayed with me a few days. We hit bars and eventually came across this gorgeous woman, six feet tall and sexy as shit. She and Kfir hit it off. Turns out, she used to be a man and had undergone reassignment surgery, she enjoyed sharing all that with him because he wowed her with those eyes."

Jarret sent Pitch a look I recognized. I also loved those eyes.

"Eventually, she got into the SUV with him to mess around. Ivan was drunk and pissed to not be involved and he got behind the wheel and started the truck. I jumped in the front seat too—I mean, hell, my ride was leaving. Those two started to argue and it got ugly. The woman wanted out of the truck. Kfir made her stay and the shouting got more and more violent. It happened pretty fast, but Ivan drove the truck to a deserted area and the whole while, Kfir's trying to convince this enormous woman to calm down, that he has it under control. When Ivan pulled down a country lane and turned off the car, she tried to get out. Turns out, she's as strong as a man when frightened, because it took all three of us to keep her in the car. Kfir eventually ended her to shut her up."

"That was woman number one," I stated, feeling horrible for the victim, but still trying to understand. "In Buffalo?" He nodded, but mostly looked at his captain. I hadn't researched the murders outside of my area, but if I did, I'm sure I'd find this poor woman's story. "Did you do the rape, the tongue, the works?" I asked low, as a scientist.

"It was sloppy, but yes. After that, Ivan and I realized this was the therapy we needed. K refused to join us, fucking traitor. Brothers stick together, but he had a woman at home by then and he didn't want Ivan near her..." Jarret glanced at me and looked away. "He wanted liaisons, said he didn't need the thrill like we did."

No one spoke a moment and I had no idea what to ask next. Pitch had a question and it was a good one.

"Kfir said he stopped. It sounds like you've stopped. Only Ivan is still at it?"

"Right. K hasn't gone out for one of these dates in weeks. I stopped because of the Maker. I'm not mad at those bitches anymore. David showed me my peace is here, with the God of the mortals. With *God*."

I shivered and looked up requesting Pitch's eye. "Maybe Keifer stopped because of what he's learned here. Everything he's saying matches up..."

Pitch held my eye, and something happened. What was it? I don't know if it has a name, but my scalp shrunk, my head rushed, and my stomach flipped. The reciprocal shine in that eye-lock told me he felt the same thing. I didn't want to break the spell, so I held position. Pitch did, too, and after four long seconds of silence, the corner of his mouth tucked in and he arched his eyebrows.

"It took Kfir several weeks to realize we were tailing him and finishing off his dates." Jarret shrugged.

"Go on," Pitch said, his voice flat, giving me the impression he was asking for my benefit.

Jarret looked to Pitch and held his eye. "I did what you would have told me to do—I kept Ivan preoccupied. He's so hung up on Kfir, worse than you ever saw when you lived together. I held him close, spoiled him, day and night. Then he wanted a camera in K's apartment. We set it up. K was fine with it, to help Ivan separate, he said. Then he'd bring his dates home and me and Ivan would watch." Jarret made a *shew* noise. "Ivan grew so incensed watching him fuck that we couldn't *help* but track the woman down and end her. We had to. There was no stopping him."

Pitch shook his head and put an arm about my shoulders, eyes to Jarret. The move meant the world to me but I held my focus.

"Letting him end these women saved you and K a lot of trouble," he said low. "You should thank me."

"I'll knock you unconscious, how's that?" Pitch said with an edge.

"The police are tracking a serial killer of transwomen. All of these in the paper were women Kiefer slept with?" I asked amazed at my dispassionate tone.

Jarret nodded. "He attracted them. They *loved him*. He said the right thing and had the right look. That hair, those lips, *fuck.*" Jarret fell silent and Pitch was looking off again in thought.

My mind raced back to my calendar. The year we were together, my lover was seeking and screwing transwomen. Is that because I asked him not to sleep with girls? In his mind, was he keeping his vow? There was a psychology missing but I was losing my confidence in the Rakum

212

model. Hell, could I have been wasting my time trying to help them?

"Wrap it up, *fuck,*" Pitch hissed. "Fuck, torture, tongue was you three in that order."

Pitch spoke his summary with no emotion, and I forgot for a moment that he'd only been human a year. None of this horrified him.

"The three of you are Patient 7, but Ivan's the one who's gone rogue."

"That's what David thinks." Jarret didn't look at me, his eyes on Pitch's face.

There's your answer, Ruth, my doctor self said inside. *You'll never make them mortal. You have to teach them to assimilate. Teach them to play mortals, to perform as a human, for the rest of their lives. Give them skills to succeed in a world where there are no vampires.*

I slowed my breathing, working this out, and Pitch looked upon me, still standing close with his arm across my shoulders.

"Where are they now?" Pitch asked still looking at me.

Jarret hemmed but said low, "Ivan has a hideaway. He takes some of his victims there. Dismembers and hides their bodies." He peeked at me and then back to Pitch. "_____" he said in their language and I whipped my face to Pitch's.

"Hmm," Pitch replied and gave a slow nod.

Jarret continued speaking and this time, Pitch did not force him to speak English. I watched and waited, growing more and more tense until finally, Pitch sighed and turned me bodily toward the door.

Jarret gave directions in English of how to find the place and said, "David and Darcy are headed there. They want to handle it. Get there first. Before he…" He tipped

213

his chin my way. "You shouldn't take her there."

"What?" I asked and allowed Pitch to walk me to the car. "What?"

I must have asked "what" fourteen times, but Pitch waited until we were underway, heading away from the church. Then he asked for my phone. I handed it over, thinking he wanted to make a call, but instead, he flung it out the window. We had reached interstate speed and with my mouth open, I jerked my face rearward.

"Pitch! What the fuck!"

"Ivan has your friend Jenny. If you want to be part of the solution, you'll need your calmest behavior."

Panic flooded my frame. It wasn't easy but after screaming curses at my driver and cursing Ivan to the root, I took a deep breath and counted to three. I wanted to help her. I loved her. She was my only friend, really, all the family I had in the world.

"What about Tiff?" I asked, my nose full of snot.

"He didn't say. It's a thirty-minute drive and Walker and Darcy will be there first."

"Why did you throw my phone?" I asked, softly cry-talking.

"Because you're human. You'll call for help." He shot me a glance, but it was loving, not judgmental. "You won't need help. I am here to protect you—Ivan and Kfir could never best me in a fight. If she's alive, Walker and Darcy will keep her alive. I told Jarret to tell them we're coming."

"Jenny," I whispered. "Why her? She has nothing to do with the Rakum. She doesn't know any of you..."

"Jarret insists he acted alone and doesn't know why," Pitch answered in a cautious tone. "My guess is Ivan's jealousy is aimed now at you." Pitch flashed me a look. "Dr. Flank—your friend. Dr. Jenny Kirkland—also your

214

friend. With the blanks we have filled in tonight, we can surmise Kfir was working his way back to you. Away from his old life…"

Pitch stopped sharing and I sensed something of his thoughts; maybe I would resume my relationship with Keifer. Maybe everything between Pitch and me was only to bring me full circle. At the moment, with my eyes filling with tears for Jenny and myself and Pitch all together, I honestly didn't have the answer.

Pitch's right hand began digging in his door pocket. I watched and wondered until he grabbed what he sought.

"It's going to be okay," he said, just like a hero in a romantic thriller. He opened his hand and I took the item. It was a tissue.

I believed him then and we barreled through the night. Watching the black landscape zoom past, I sought solace inside, imagining the Jesus picture, the one I spoke to as a child, sad, sore, and afraid. I asked Him to help me, to help Jenny, and as I thought of all that had transpired the past few days, I did begin to feel better. To be more precise, I felt hopeful, like we would arrive and Jenny would be fine, Keifer would be normal, and Ivan would be punished for his crimes.

Pitch cleared his throat and I looked over. We met eyes and my heart swelled. Something happened to him, this was a different man—if I compared photographs of him from Session One to now?

"Your switch-hitter was Ivan," he said in a soft tone, apologizing with his eyes. "When you bought the house together, just like at his earlier place, Ivan installed cameras with Kfir's blessing. But it seems you grew close and Kfir insisted they be removed."

My eyes could not have been larger as Pitch explained

with gentle short phrases. I gathered from the timing that this is what Jarret had been telling him before we left. I waited for him to continue and he did, still with sorrow.

"The camera over the bed was Ivan's. Kfir did not know about it. I thought you should know."

"I found it. That's why I came to your house. I was devastated…" My voice trickled away and Pitch gave me a small nod.

That night, when I awoke and thought a stranger had been in my bed, my lover's expression was as I first thought: true surprise. I exhaled and blew my nose.

"And the glove," Pitch said interrupting my thoughts.

He looked away with purpose. *With guilt?*

"You asked if I loaned out my gloves. I blew it off. Remember?"

His voice strained, still avoiding my eye. It was *regret*…

"Yeah…"

"I loaned them to Ivan. I never got them back. I had my suspicions about him from the start, but when you asked, I wasn't where I am now." He huffed at his own words. "I had no idea you'd been played."

I reached across to touch his forearm. "I understand. I really do." I was trying to comfort him. Where was my own paranoia? My fear for Jenny? It was melting. She was going to be okay.

"There's the turn. Follow my lead."

I said I would and Pitch slowed at the T-junction to roll to a stop. He looked over fully to hold my gaze.

"Kfir would never come against me. Also, me, David, and Darcy can prevent any harm from coming to you. We want to keep Jenny alive, but be prepared. She's probably dead." He sounded truly sorry and with my eyes watering, I gave him a nod.

216

"I think she's okay," I whispered, and Pitch said he hoped so. He resumed the final leg of the drive and I watched out the windshield for a structure.

Inside I imagined Jesus and those eyes. *"Tell Me what's wrong. If I can help, I will…"*

Somehow, deep down, I knew He was going to do His best.

The Showdown

van's hideaway was barely a building. What appeared to be an Airstream trailer from fifty years ago had been shored up with plywood and two by fours and covered with corrugated steel. As we approached rolling slowly across a road made of forest leaves and not gravel, we made out a white van on the north side of the unit. A black BMW and Darcy's familiar red truck also sat on either side of the trail. No lights burned in the windows, although it was obvious, even in the waning light of dusk, that they were caked with the film of age and disuse.

Pitch pulled in behind Darcy's truck. My eyes fell to my purse in the floorboard. *My handgun.* I hadn't fired it in three years and hadn't cleaned it either. But it was loaded. I turned to Pitch.

"I have a gun," I said in a whisper. "Do you want to take it?"

He shook his head. "It won't come to that. Rakum don't need guns amongst their brethren," he said with a little smile. "Add this to your studies. Let's show Doctor

Angleton how Pitch handles his subordinates."

With one last game smile, he put his fingers to the door handle. I mimicked his actions and we exited the car together and looked at each other over the hood.

"Where are they?" I asked and we both trained our eyes to the structure. "I don't hear them, either."

"They're out there. I imagine in the back out of sight. Stay close."

We began the trek toward the trailer and I stepped practically in Pitch's footprints. I listened so intently that my ears popped and the darkness thickened as we stepped into the shade of the structure. The sun had been down an hour and night was full upon us. A half-moon gave little illumination but at least the skies were clear.

At the corner of the trailer, Pitch held up his hand to get me to stop and he peeked to the backyard. It was wooded with no clearing to speak of. I peeked around his shoulder and caught a glimpse of a flashlight beam cutting through the night, bouncing off trees and leaves and limbs.

Pitch pressed his back to the structure and I did the same. Then he turned his face to mine. He didn't appear frightened or worried and this gave me courage.

"See the Magnolia?" he whispered and I trained my eyes the way he indicated. "I suspect from that tree trunk, we'll have a better look at my brothers' positions."

I didn't doubt him; he'd done surreptitious work as a Rakum captain for centuries, his movements comfortable and unhurried.

"David and Darcy will talk Ivan down. Kfir is one I'll have to watch." Pitch sucked his teeth and sighed.

Before Last Assembly, the entire Rakum race worked as a unit, pursuing common goals, and it ran seamlessly and without issue beneath mortal radar for three thousand years. Only after God entered the picture did they have angst against each other.

"One last warning," he said in a very kind tone, his eyes on the dark trees, "whether she's dead or alive, Jenny has no doubt been tortured. Do not scream. Do not react. There will be time for that after we have Ivan restrained."

I agreed with a nod. Although I was not an MD, I'd attended cadaver and trauma studies. I was not squeamish, never had been. But I still believed Jenny was okay.

Pitch gave me a final nod and turned to walk quietly toward the trees.

Within minutes, I heard voices. At first, David Walker speaking their language, his inflection that of one counseling a man off a ledge. Then I heard Darcy in the lulls, and although I didn't understand, he was backing up whatever the preacher was saying. Ivan's voice rang out interlaced in their remarks and he was screeching, his words hard and guttural. The hairs on my arm stood up and I scooched closer behind Pitch.

I imagined Jesus and His eyes from that picture on the wall and I knew He was listening from wherever He was. I asked Him again to make *Jenny be safe. Please let Jenny be safe.*

"Kazak!" Pitch called out and then spoke a few sentences in their language. Then he said in English, "Ruth is with me. I'm coming in."

"Ruth?"

Kiefer's voice. He appeared, breaking between tight branches of a natural hedge before us.

"Ruth! What in the world! You shouldn't be here!" Kiefer came forward and Pitch held up his hand.

"That's far enough," he said with a threat.

Kiefer obeyed but turned his face to mine. "You shouldn't be here." He glanced behind him and then back to Pitch. "You know who is in there, right?"

I looked between both men and then at the bushes, mountainous in the low light.

"Jenny?" I shouted with a question mark and then louder, "Jenny!"

From somewhere in front of us, a tiny feminine voice asked for help.

Pitch jumped into action. In a blur of movement, he grabbed Kiefer by the forearm, jerked him close to me, and caused his hand to hold my wrist. "Stand right here and protect your fucking mate," he said with a caustic hiss. Then he looked to me and said softer, "Stay here." Next, he disappeared into the brush.

Kiefer moved his grip to my upper arm and gave it a squeeze. "What are you doing with him? Are you together now?"

After all that had transpired and with worry escalating for Jenny, I didn't answer. I kept my eyes on the place Pitch disappeared. Kiefer continued to question me as I strained to hear past the shrubbery. I called Jenny's name again.

"It's too late for her," Kiefer said and also looked that way. "You shouldn't have come. I was taking care of this. I was gonna fix everything."

I pulled away, in the direction Pitch had gone. "Jenny!" I called again. Keifer's contact followed and he provided resistance. I couldn't move forward.

The men argued on the other side, each man's voice battling with angry shouts, none of them in English. Then I heard sounds of surprise and of violence. I needed to get in there. I was unable to jerk free of Keifer's grip, so I dropped to the ground. The move surprised him enough that he released in order to secure me another way. I used that moment to scoot on my hands and knees into the bushes. I could not have prepared myself for what I saw.

My eyes instinctively went to my friend, tied between two trees, nude, her skin dyed crimson by blood shed from multiple wounds that were too small to see from my position. In my peripheral vision, Pitch, David, and Darcy faced Ivan, brandishing a serrated hunting blade. He stood with his back to my friend, twenty feet from where she hang. I made a decision.

In a bolt, I returned through the bushes, past Keifer, dodging his reach, and I shot for the hideaway. I ran to Pitch's Lexus and dove into the passenger side floorboard. I fished through my purse. When I had my gun in hand, I held it to the light of the rising moon to check the load indicator—a round was chambered. This model's safety was in the grip, so I fitted it into my hand and pointed it to the ground for the jog back to the commotion.

Keifer was not in sight as I skirted the greenery more than before, planning to emerge close to Jenny's trees. As quietly as possible, I pushed through the hedge, ignoring scratches to my exposed skin and brambles that pulled at my long hair, and came up to Jenny sideways. She was only semi-conscious either from blood loss or trauma and I wanted to get her down. With the gun in my shooting hand, I pointed it to where Ivan stood still arguing with his brothers.

With my eye flitting between Jenny's bindings and the four men, I worked furiously with one hand to unhook her wrist. Ivan had used wire and it cut through her flesh causing rivulets down the tree. But he had used twist-tie closure with heavy gauge wire so I was able to undo it with one hand. When the first binding came loose, I moved in front of her and her upper body draped partially over my shoulder. I jumped to the other wrist, but realized if I undid

222

it, she'd be hanging by her ankles, doing more harm than good.

Oh God! I hadn't thought of that. I stopped what I was doing and shouted for help.

Pitch glanced up and met my eye, shaking his head in a small movement. Ivan spun around, looking as if he didn't realize I was there. What had he thought Pitch meant when he yelled out his warning? But then I knew. I read it all in Ivan's gaze. He had lost his mind, and it had nothing to do with being a former vampire. This was plain old human *lunacy*.

Ivan swiveled to surge in my direction and all three Rakum followed after him, Keifer the only one out of sight. Darcy and Pitch reached him first and each grabbed Ivan by an arm. He was easy to immobilize although Ivan struggled in their grip, screaming epithets at me, at them, and at Jenny.

I still had my gun pointed at Ivan.

"Put down the gun, Ruth," Darcy said in a booming voice. "No need for that." His voice carried with it a command, as if I was his subordinate. I looked at Pitch. His opinion, I cared more about, and he gave me a half nod. His gaze read, *we have this in hand. Help Jenny.*

I sought David's eye. "I need help!" I yelled to the preacher when he looked over. David circumnavigated Pitch and Darcy struggling to keep Ivan in place. "Help me get her down!"

David moved to her ankles. I was suddenly shoved from behind with gusto and I hit the ground hard, the gun bouncing away as I fell.

"Let Ivan go!" Keifer said walking up to stand beside me. He lifted my gun and held it in hand. "Let him go now."

I tried to rise but Kiefer grunted for me to stay put. He put his boot to my back between my shoulder blades, holding me down. I could see his brothers, Pitch and Darcy having words in their language over Ivan's head. Then, Darcy took full custody so Pitch could face off with Keifer.

"Hand over the gun," he said to Kiefer, his chin lowered. He took two steps toward us and stopped. I was terrified then that Keifer might shoot and I called for Pitch to take cover.

"Why do you care?" Kiefer asked Pitch. "Have you stepped into my shoes? I was working it out. You know I was. I told you I was working it out."

"Give me the gun, Kfir," Pitch said in a low voice. He repeated similar-sounding words in their language prompting Keifer to also respond in kind. He did not lower the weapon.

During this showdown, David had frozen in place, having undid Jenny's ankles and lowered her to the ground. He had also draped his outer coat across her shoulders, but she was not doing well, now fully unconscious and leaning against him, her head lolling. David's eyes were huge and that's when I noticed his lips were moving. Was he praying? Not so deep down, I hoped that he was.

"Are you with him?" Kiefer asked me I assume, although I couldn't see his face the way I was positioned against the wet leaves. "Tell me now."

"Let me up," I said in a grunt pushing against the ground with both palms. Keifer increased his weight. I wasn't going anywhere.

"Are you with him?" he asked with gravel in his voice.

"I'm sure as hell not with you," I said angry and mimicking his tone.

Pitch took another step in our direction and I watched

his face, my expression begging him to be careful. Kiefer sounded unbalanced, unstable. Pitch assured me that he could control his brethren as a Rakum, but how would mortal-Pitch control a mortal brother who had lost his mind?

"Keifer, please stop," I said forcing a normal voice, one I used when the world wasn't falling down around me. "This isn't you. You don't want to hurt anyone. Not your brothers, not me, not my friend. You're just upset that we broke up. All that is normal. You're okay, it's all going to be okay, trust me."

"Dr. Ruth has spoken, brothers!" Keifer said in reply, his face downward by the volume of his voice. "I suppose your diagnosis is that I'm acting out of jealousy, eh? This is how mortals deal with deceitful mates and treachery among his closest allies?"

My mind raced with a myriad of responses and I had to choose one. Considering Keifer currently pointed a gun at the man who *now* meant the world to me, I prayed in my heart that I would choose the right one.

"Exactly, Keef. Exactly. This is exactly how we get, how humans behave," I rasped as he hadn't lessened his weight. "Lots of men and women take up weapons against their mates, but it doesn't have to end with pulling the trigger. It can end with everyone hugging it out, ready to face the new day…"

"What if I'd rather end you *and* my traitor-brothers, and then face the new day?" he asked and I didn't think he expected a reply. I had one, though, and I spat it out in the calmest tone I could muster.

"But they're not traitors. It's just a disagreement. They love you, they want you to prosper. They want you to be happy."

"This is a fucking funny way of showing it," he replied and adjusted his aim from Pitch's sternum to his head. "Steal my woman while I work out the shit that's ruining our mate-up? I came here tonight with Ivan to set Jenny free." Keifer removed his foot from my back but when I pushed upward with my hands, he replaced it. "You and David have only known me a few months. But Pitch and Darcy? They should have trusted that I know what I'm doing. Last night in your apartment," he said to Pitch, "I told you. I told you I was busy straightening out Ivan before Ruth came after me like she did. You didn't help. You let me go and went after her instead."

I recalled the video of Keifer drunk-talking to Pitch, inviting him to paint the town red. It didn't sound like he'd been sharing his plan to rescue Jenny.

"No, you told me you were giving up, you were done trying to be human," Pitch said low and advanced another step. Again, I begged with my eyes for him to stay back.

"Spin it like a mortal, perfect," Keifer answered.

Behind Pitch, Ivan shouted in Rakum Hungarian (I assume) and Pitch commanded in English that he be silent.

"Ruth is right," David said behind me, still on his knees, now blocking Jenny with his body. "None of this is unfixable. Yeshua[11] is here with us. This isn't you. Put down the gun and let's fix this the Rakum way."

"Oh, so we're Rakum again?" Keifer barked without moving his eyes from Pitch. "Make up your mind, David. Are we men or Rakum?"

"We're both, you idiot," Darcy's voice sounded from the furthest away. "You'll always be a Rakum. There's no erasing us, your brothers, our fellowship stands forever. Put down the gun and let us resume our assimilation. You're pissing me off."

Darcy's deep vibrato filled the small clearing and I wondered if I wasn't the only one getting chills at the sound.

"Don't make me fucking disarm you, Kfir," Pitch said low, his evil tone giving me goosebumps of a different sort.

"Keifer," I said straining, "you and I are over, that's true, but you've lived through *centuries*. Why would you allow this to matter so much? You'll live another fifty years and have hundreds of ups and downs…" I paused, aware my words were harsh, but the truth of them was what I had learned (I hope) that the Rakum react to best. "Breaking up with a woman is not the end of the world. Think about it."

"Drop the gun and let's pretend you never turned a weapon on your brother," David said, and I watched Pitch's face. He gave an agreeing nod.

One, two, three seconds elapsed and with a robotic jerk, Keifer lowered his gun hand, removed his foot from my back, and stooped to place the gun beside my fingers. I scrambled to stand, and when up, I dusted off my front, gun in hand, the barrel pointed down. I backed to David and dropped to the ground to check Jenny, keeping a wary eye on the others.

"Come close," Pitch said in a soft voice and Keifer strode into him without delay, chest to chest.

The energy of the clearing grew decidedly more calm and I handed the gun to David and checked Jenny's vitals.

"We need to get her to a hospital," I said low.

David nodded, but turned his eyes to his brethren. Pitch and Keifer were still in a clutch, but now they were eye to eye and murmuring below my hearing.

"Pitch," Darcy said across the space. "Get over here. Use that trick you showed me. Put him out." Darcy held

Ivan with hands to his biceps from behind, and their insane brother continued to wriggle and spout curses. "Let's get him to the church."

Jenny was still unconscious, but she began to shiver and her teeth chattered. David's jacket only covered her shoulders to her pubic bone. I jerked off my Northface and draped it across her lap and thighs.

"She needs to get warm," I said facing Pitch. *"Now!"*

Darcy walked Ivan bodily toward Pitch and Keifer and the man screamed curses. I heard him saying Keifer's name in there, and it brought to mind his original problem—he was obsessed with Keifer. I turned to tell Pitch to remember that, but at the same time, Darcy lost his grip on the maniac, who thrust himself upwards with both feet to escape to one side.

"Motherfucking-shit-hole!" he yelled all but galloping full speed into Keifer and Pitch. Almost there, he ducked low to lift something from the ground, and when he reached them, he thrust his previously discarded blade into the moonlight. David leapt forward from his kneeling position to my right and jumped toward his brethren. On the other side of the space, Darcy also moved into the cluster.

Whump. Whump. Whump.

The distinctive sound of the knife driving home into flesh reached my ears and I worked to get Jenny off the ground. She weighed barely 130 pounds, but I wasn't strong enough to lift her off the wet leaves. Dragging her by her armpits, not able to care that my jacket fell off her legs, I yelled for Pitch to be careful. The group of men struggled as a unit in the dark, the half-moon allowing fuzzy shadows on the wet ground. Pulling Jenny through the bushes was harder than I expected, and a portion of my hair was yanked out by a final spastic move to fling us free to the other side.

The men were shouting in their language and my heart cried out to God that Pitch would not be injured. Running backward, I did not fall as I pulled my friend's form across the yard. All the way to Pitch's car, Jenny did not awaken. When I opened the back door to fold her into the seat, I rejoiced at the sight of the keys in the ignition.

"Thank you, Pitch!" I said in the car, finding my place behind the wheel. "Thank you, God!"

When the engine turned over and I got the car in gear, I paused, watching the quiet Airstream trailer.

Pitch! What if he's hurt? What if Ivan stabs him? Or Darcy? Or David? Or... What if?

Behind me, Jenny whimpered a small sound and I got into motion. God had kept Jenny alive. He could keep Pitch safe, too. I prayed for that very thing and zoomed my friend toward town.

The New Day

I knew the precise location of Ivan's hideaway, but when questioned by police, I claimed that I found her slumped on the shoulder of Highway 31. She could tell them more later and this would give Pitch and the others time to clear out. Jenny would make a full recovery, her wounds shallow and intended to cause pain and fear, not death.

Tiffany had been out of town, which was why I couldn't reach her when I was freaking out. When I checked Jenny into the hospital and provided her information, they got Tiff on the first try. She came down and she and I held each other as the physicians stitched Jenny's worst wounds. Before they put her down for a much-needed nap, she asked for me.

"How did you find me?" she asked, her eyes wide with true wonder.

I hadn't realized she'd been conscious any of that time in the woods and I wondered then what all she remembered. Had she seen Pitch? Or Keifer? I sincerely hoped not because none of them needed the spotlight the abduction could bring if Jenny remembered them.

I'll ask. What the hell?

With Tiff on her other side, holding Jenny's hand, I asked, "Who did this? What happened?"

Jenny shook her head once. "I don't know. I was walking to my truck and I got knocked out." She looked at her wife who leaned low and kissed her forehead.

When she returned her gaze to me, she looked strong. Not like a woman tortured and hung to a tree for thirty-six hours, which is how long I overheard the police captain say in the hallway earlier.

"Like I told the police, it was a man, but he wore a mask. He was white and six feet, but the rest?" She shook her head. "I saw where we went. I drew them a map."

The nurse came in then and asked us to let her sleep. I kissed her cheek and sat with Tiff another hour before deciding to head to my own house.

I didn't have a phone since Pitch tossed mine away, so in the hospital, I stopped at the pharmacy and picked up a cheap cell. I walked to where I'd parked Pitch's car and climbed in. Once the new phone was plugged in to the charging station, I directed it to contact the Cloud. For fifteen minutes, my phone filled with saved information and when it chimed complete, I punched Pitch's saved icon.

"Please, please, please," I whispered in the car, but unlike a month ago, today I was speaking to God. It felt okay.

I had assigned a new phone number; maybe Pitch wouldn't pick up because of that. Maybe he was dead in the woods? Maybe.

"Yes?" a man's voice barked.

It sounded sort of like Pitch, but was it?

They mimic so well... I thought with traces of what Jenny

231

would call PTSD.

But I survived...

"Ruth?" he said and this time, I had no doubt of his identity.

"Pitch! Oh my God! Are you okay? Is everyone okay?"

"I'm okay. Where are you?" he asked, his voice somber.

"Baptist East, Montgomery. You?" I asked my tone dropping to match. Something was wrong.

"Home. Columbus. Will you come here?" he asked, his voice flat.

"Yes, of course, I'll leave now," I replied and pressed the ignition switch. I brought up the GPS in the dash and began entering Pitch's home address from memory. 160 miles. Three hours. *Shit.* "What's wrong?"

"Nothing, just come. I'll watch for you," he said and I got on the road, inside trying to guess what he wouldn't say.

"Is Darcy okay? David? Keifer?" I asked weaving my way through traffic. "You sound upset."

"Can we speak in person?" he asked and now he sounded like Keifer.

Or just sweet, like Kiefer use to sound on the phone.

Or maybe Pitch was still morphing. He said he'd been talking to the Maker. That he was changing. Our every conversation—good and bad—returned to mind as I reached the interstate.

"Yes, I'm coming. I'll be there in three."

Pitch said *good* and hung up.

What followed was the longest drive of my life. The sun was sitting on the horizon as I pulled through Pitch's wide iron gate demarcating his plantation abode. I drove down the driveway as long as any on *Gone with the Wind* and when I reached the parking area, I pulled to the front door. Pitch stepped to the porch to meet me, a crutch tucked into his right armpit.

"What happened?" I asked shimmying free of the seatbelt to scramble from the car. "What? What?"

I reached him and with my palms to his outer arms, I scanned his bandaged leg wrapped with thick gauze from mid-thigh to below the knee.

"Give me a fucking kiss," he said, making a single bounce on his good foot, as if getting close.

I grinned and did so, sliding my hands up to cup his face, his beard soft under my fingers. A simple peck multiplied to two, three and the fourth one was longer. Our heads tipped to opposite directions and the kiss opened, him balancing on one foot plus the crutch, and me still holding his cheeks.

"Damn, you're sexy as shit," he said when he pulled back an inch to breathe. "Is everything you do so fucking provoking?"

I only smiled, a shake to my head. I dropped my hands. "I don't think so. You must be infatuated with me or something," I said teasing.

Pitch snaked his non-crutch hand to my waist and pulled me snug one-armed. "I am in love with you," he said low and kissed me again.

The words circled my mind as I went along, matching his effort until he again needed to breathe. I wanted him to feel that way, but he was a Rakum. Darcy said it in the clearing—the fact that I had been missing the whole while. I wanted to help them assimilate; I was honestly and sincerely interested in their success, but I did not need to make them human.

I only needed to help them be "like" humans.

That would be enough.

Did Pitch love me as a mortal or a Rakum?

"What the fuck is taking you so long to say it back?" he said, a twinkle in his beautiful eyes. "I know you love me. You've had a boner for me since Day One."

I grinned at his words. "Nuh-uh, not that asshole," I said and shook my head. "I got it the night you drove me to the church. You showed me a new side."

"My good-Pitch side, eh?" he said, his strong arm gripping me so steady and looking down on me with emotions larger than we understood. "So, say it, woman."

I smiled again, holding his eye. I then pursed my lips and dropped my gaze to my hands, both of which were sliding up his shirt over his pectoral muscle. I loved him. He knew it. Why wouldn't I say it out loud? I was going to, right? What was I protecting?

"I love you, too, Pitch," he said in my voice, so much like me that I laughed out loud. He continued, "You sexy man-beast. Take me to bed, you broke-leg, half-human, asshole, and fuck me blue."

I laughed again and shook my head. I exhaled and leaned in, pressing my lips to his beard. I remained there, close and breathed him in, his cologne, his shampoo, his everything. When I released my breath, I said against his cheek, "I love you, Pitch. Forever love. And all the shit I went through to get here today, I think was for this. I think you are my reward."

Pitch was quiet and then his arm shifted to stroking my back in welcome swaths, one after the other.

"So, Ruth Angleton, you love me and I love you," he said in his own sultry voice, spoken low and over my head. "Let's fuck."

I laughed and leaned away. "Try it romantic-like," I

said with humor. My answer was yes, and he knew it. This was a new thing, we were starting new, our relationship clock clicked to Start the moment he said he loved me.

"Romantic-like," he repeated in a thoughtful tone. He kissed my forehead and leaned out to see my face. "Come to bed." He grinned when I did. "Shit, Ruth," he said in a kind chuckle. "I'm two-hundred and twenty years old, all that time a fucking malcontent. I'm growing, but this might be as romantic as I get."

"You are wonderful," I said then and moved in for a new kiss. "Please, Pitch, take me to bed."

His grin widened and with a nod, he hobbled into a turn for the door. I walked beside him, chuckling at his clumsy use of the single crutch. When we reached his bedroom, he dropped the item and hopped on one leg to the mattress.

He looked at me with a smile. "What's so funny, princess? Get over here and I'll give you something to laugh about."

My eyes widened at his words and when he had a moment, his did too.

"Fuck it, Ruth!" he said and waved both arms in a grabby gesture, all the while stranded by his injury to the bed. "Come close!"

With more peace than I had felt in a very long time, I did. I folded into Pitch's arms and let him run the show. This was a man I knew, both sides, up and down, wrong and right. I'd seen him before, during, and after his new growth, and he had watched me mature in different ways as well. In the following minutes, he had me nearly disrobed and I told him to wait.

"Wait?" he said in a rasp, stripping off his shirt at the same time. "Wait?"

I grinned, breathing as hard as he was. "Let's decide what we want to do before we go any further."

"Okay, let's," he agreed but fell in close to lave my neck.

"Trust me, it will be best to know," I said and waited for him to come out to see me. "Let's decide."

"I don't follow," he said but his eyes read that he wanted to.

"I want a relationship with you, I want to shoot for a lifetime. What do you want?" It was risky, but with Rakum, I expected him to be honest. I hadn't done this with Kiefer or any other man, but it seemed I had matured enough to do so now. Maybe Pitch had, too.

"I want you for life, Ruth," he said and lowered his chin, eyes up. "You and me? We're compatible."

He was right, we were, in every way. He resumed sucking my neck and I had to clarify the last item. It would make the sex better, but mostly, tomorrow's sex, too.

"And I want you and I to be exclusive. Monogamous. No sex with any other living beings," I said in his hair since his face was lowering to my breasts.

"That is what I want, too," he said, his lips now to my nipple.

That was good enough.

He meant it and now he knew what I expected and what I wanted. I want him and him alone. Pitch propped to his elbows and maneuvered his mass to drape across my middle.

"The most beautiful woman in the entire world, and she's all mine," he said, the awe in his voice genuine.

I would take his word for it.

And he was wonderful.

25

The Man with the Eye-Patch

ithin two months, I had moved to Pitch's plantation and we made it our home. For now, I'm not working, but when we finish traveling the world, we might settle down and have a baby. I'm thirty and I know the clock is ticking. I still have a desire to help Pitch's brothers assimilate, so I suspect we'll do an informal thing here at the house, sort of what David does for them spiritually on his property, we will do for their mental and emotional issues here.

Darcy and David weren't injured in Ivan's knife attack. Pitch took a deep gash to the femoral artery, but didn't bleed out because of Darcy's excellent medical knowledge. Today, David still runs the church in Tuscaloosa and Darcy lives in Atlanta, still visiting several times a week. Pitch thinks he's looking for a wife, but I haven't heard any updates on that. He is coming to visit us next week and you can be sure I will snoop into his business.

Keifer moved to the church property as a deacon of sorts. During Ivan's attack, he had moved in front of David to protect him and caught the hilt of the knife to his face.

His eyeball was irreparably ruptured. Pitch says Keifer bought the best prosthetic eye money could buy, but he prefers to wear an eye patch and say, "Arrrr!" when people make note of it. A phone update from Polly Anna revealed that he was dating again, that he had gotten serious with one of his brothers from a different pack. I think that's good for him. I told her to give him my best and I hope he isn't mad at me.

And Ivan? The night he went crazy, they took him back to the church and in a detailed ceremony that involved the Rakum from the original Rabbit debacle—Michael Stone, an Elder named Roman, and a brother named Javier—they prayed over him until he returned to normal. Polly Anna says he's as right as rain, and when I asked Pitch, he agreed.

So that is the story of the Malcontent, now the sexiest and most wonderful husband in the world. Tomorrow, we fly to Greece and from there, I'm not sure. One thing I am certain of is that I learned something *huge* over that horrible time; everything I suffered in my life was used to help other people in different ways. I think about that when giving advice to Pitch's brothers. It is a great feeling, helping people be happy.

On that note, I'll go see what Pitch is up to. You'd be surprised how funny he is, how relaxed. Geez. Life is good. Thank God for Pitch!

Where the Rabbit Characters were born…

NOTE to Emil's Readers: *Emil writes Ellen C. Maze's characters with her full cooperation. Ellen's novels have fewer "F-words" but grow progressively dark and mature as the plot delves into the Rakum/vampire's mindset. Book One, below, is a strong PG-13. ~ BatyaD, Ed., RRB*

140 5-star Reviews Across the Series
2020 Reader's Favorite Gold Medal Winner

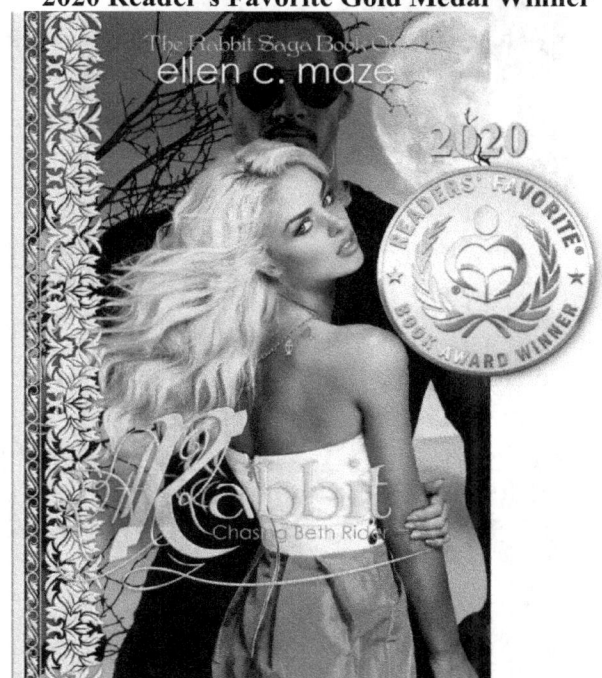

Rabbit: Chasing Beth Rider Book One of the Rabbit Saga
Ellen C Maze

More from Emil Jersey

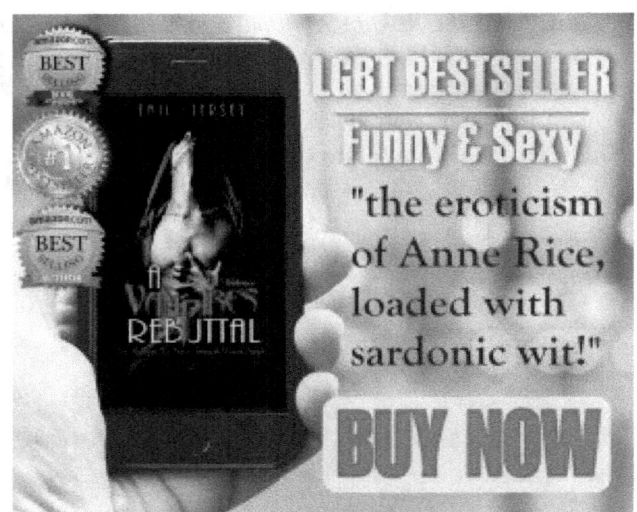

Jersey tells his story (and some of Darcy's) in:

Blood Sex & Violence, A Vampire's Rebuttal by
Emil Jersey (Run Rabbit Books 2019)
EARNED 3 5-STAR CRITICAL REVIEWS from
Readers' Favorite!

Darcy Vandiver woos you with his complete memoir, also winning a 5-star Reader's Favorite seal!

A suitable read for fans of LGBTQ and steamy romance, this book is an engrossing tale filled with likable characters. The lead character, Darcy, is opinionated and intelligent [and he] shares his story in an arresting first-person narrative that pulls the reader in from the first page.

The descriptions are terrific and Jersey's gift for character is exemplified in each chapter... taking the reader on a sensual journey into the heart of Darcy Vandiver, the master's favorite. Enjoy!

Title:	Darcy Vandiver, Vampire Sexpert, A Memoir
Subtitle:	The Rabbit Saga Collection
Author:	Emil Jersey
Genre:	Fiction - LGBTQ

5-stars
Reviewed by Christian Sia

See on Amazon: https://www.amazon.com/dp/B08717B32F

Endnotes

---

[1] The Bankers, Guap and Polly, controlled the wealth of the Rakum Fathers, as introduced in *Anomaly: Beyond the Rabbit,* Book Four of the Rabbit Saga by Ellen C Maze. https://www.amazon.com/gp/product/B07KRZYW7T?notRedirectToSDP=1&ref_=dbs_mng_calw_3&storeType=ebooks

[2] *Rabbit: Chasing Beth Rider* (Book One of Six in the series) tells the story of the Rakum, leading to the saga that continues to this day (the novel is sold on Amazon under the same name, by Ellen C Maze).

[3] Beth Rider-Stone is a woman all the Rakum know because of what she accomplished at Last Assembly to turn their world upside-down.

[4] Published by Run Rabbit Books, July 2020: *Darcy Vandiver, Vampire Sexpert, a Memoir by Emil Jersey.*

[5] "Mate": Before Last Assembly, a Rakum might choose a mortal as a mate, but the arrangement was strictly for the Rakum, and only lasted as long as his interest remained.

[6] To read about that crazy time, read *Conundrum,* by Ellen C. Maze, featuring Elder Canaan and Darcy Vandiver. Link: https://www.amazon.com/dp/B081HYYMS5/ref=cm_sw_r_tw_dp_U_x_UhzVEb1HGZCBZ

[7] Ellen C. Maze, the creator of the Rabbit Saga is writing a novel entitled THE VESTIGE, and it will give readers a "where are they now" as the characters are thrown into a new plot involving the Rakum, the Elders, and their offspring. Sign up at www.ellencmaze.com to receive email alerts for this and all titles related to The Rabbit Saga and Rabbit Saga Collection!

---

[8] *Delectable and rare*, a pet name for ish-mikhan (Rakum Hungarian)

[9] In "Rabbit: Chasing Beth Rider," Rabbit Saga Book One, the Rakum enter our awareness with Beth Rider reveals their spiritual origins. More at www.ellencmaze.com or www.LittleRoniPublishers.com.

[10] Rabbit: Chasing Beth Rider, by Ellen C Maze www.ellencmaze.com

[11] "Yeshua" is the Hebrew name for Jesus. Some of the Rakum know Him in Hebrew and David is one of those.